A Tower To Heaven

Stan Johnston

First Edition

Copyright © 2021 Stan Johnston.

All rights reserved. This book or any portion thereof may not be reproduced or used in any manner whatsoever without the express written permission of the publisher except for the use of brief quotations in a book review.

Printed by IngramSpark, Inc., in the United States of America.

First printing, 2021
ISBN: 978-0-578-87106-6

byStanJohnston
5141 Loch Leven Drive
Pollock Pines, CA 95726
www.bystanjohnston.com

This is a work of fiction. Though some people, places, and events are documented in sacred and secular historical texts, all are used in a fictitious manner that is the product of the author's imagination. They are fictionalized accounts of historical persons and not actual accounts. Details also came from the archaeological, geological, and geographical history of ancient Mesopotamia.

Cover design: Petercover

Cover image: "The Tower of Babel" by Pieter Bruegel the Elder.
(Public domain. Image via Wikimedia Commons.)

Scripture taken from the New Century Version®. Copyright © 2005 by Thomas Nelson. Used by permission. All rights reserved.

For My Children:

Sara, Nathan, Rachel, and Rebeka

And Future Generations of the Promise

"What has been done will be done again.

There is nothing new under the sun."

Ecclesiastes 1:9 (NCV)

Table of Contents

Preface

Loss and Restoration

When your dreams become the next day's headlines, you start taking them seriously. It happened to me several times, which is why I knew my dream about the Tower in 1980 was more than an overactive imagination.

The dreams had started about two years earlier, while I was working as a writer and editor for a newspaper in Minnesota. Simply put, I had a series of dreams that came true – literally. I saw major current events in mental images ahead of time.

Prophetic visions did not fit into my agnostic world view at the time, but eventually I had to acknowledge the existence of something beyond the natural. I was even more surprised when I encountered an actual deity. After that, as open as I tried to be, I could accept nothing less than a *real* God.

By the time I had my dream about the Tower, I was paying attention to details. Those are recounted as Eber's experience in Chapter 1, and they remain enduring memories for me.

Despite that, decades went by before I understood the full meaning of the dream.

In 2019, God began to whisper to me about using the Tower of Babel as an allegory for this point in history – our fading faith, disruptive change in society, and human decimation of the environment. My only qualification was being a person of faith who has written about digital disruption. Also, I volunteer at an environmental education center.

I am a writer in the secular world, not a theologian or prophet. Because *A Tower to Heaven* was shaped around my personal interests, the idea seemed intriguing but not urgent. However, three months later, a virus of Biblical proportions was unleashed globally. Soon I felt the book needed to be written *now*, it had to be a *story* instead of an essay, and it could not end at the fall of the Tower or ensuing confusion.

The message is simple: Our hope is in God alone, not in buildings or even heaven.

He created humans in a perfect world, the Garden of Eden, to be his daily companions, to have loving relationships with each other, and to care for our world. Though we have turned our backs on all three roles repeatedly, God also has restored each throughout history – one generation at a time.

This feels like another moment of reckoning, driven by a deadly pandemic. That means it also is a time of restoration. I resolved to let God start that in my own heart, and it left me profoundly changed. Because of that, I deeply appreciate the many people who encouraged me while writing this book.

But I especially thank God for trusting me to be his scribe. In the end, history is always his story to write.

Soli Deo Gloria.

– Stan Johnston
February 2021

People, Places, Things

People

- **Eber** – Refused to help build the Tower.
- **Azurad** – Wife of Eber, and daughter of King Nimrod.
- **Nimrod** – King of Babylon. Mighty hunter. Builder of cities and the Tower.
- **Arpachshad** ("Arpa") – Born 2 years after The Deluge. Grandson of Noah, grandfather of Eber.
- **Peleg** – Son of Eber and Azurad. Led Second Dispersal.
- **Joktan** – Son of Eber and Azurad.
- **Lord (En) Priestess** – Princess and powerful leader of major temples dedicated to the moon god, Nanna.

Cities

- **City of Babylon** – On the Euphrates, 160 miles north of the Gulf of Dilmun.
- **City of Ur** – At the confluence of Euphrates and Gulf in ancient times, 160 miles south of Babylon.
- **Harran City** – On a tributary to the Euphrates at the base of the northern mountains, 630 miles north of Babylon.
- **Nineveh** – On the Tigris, 300 miles northeast of Babylon.

Rivers and Seas

- **The Great River** – Euphrates
- **The Arrow River** – Tigris
- **The Great Sea** – Mediterranean Sea
- **Gulf of Dilmun** – Persian Gulf

Gods and Religion

- **Marduk** – "Bull of the Sun" and king of the gods. Patron deity for the City of Babylon.
- **Nanna** – God of the moon and "Lord of Wisdom." Patron deity for the City of Ur. Lunar calendars guided life.
- **Tower of Babylon** – "Foundation of Heaven on Earth" with a temple to Marduk at its top.
- **Temple of Nanna in Ur** – "House of the Great Light" to the moon god (full moon).
- **Temple of Nanna in Harran** – "House of Joys" to the moon god (crescent moon)
- **Ni** – A "physical tingling of the flesh when seeing a deity."

Glossary

- **The Land Between** – *Mesopotamia*, the area between the Tigris and Euphrates rivers.
- **Mud Bricks** – Mud bricks dried in the sun.
- **Burnt Bricks** – Mud bricks baked in a furnace.
- **Bitumen** – Natural asphalt. A key waterproof mortar.
- **Cliffs of Najaf** – Major cliffs framing the Sea of Najaf just east of the Euphrates River.
- **The Great Ridge** -- Runs roughly east–west north of Sippar, separating northern and southern Land Between.

1

Two Dreamers

Eber felt the sea breeze on his face and smelled the saltwater Gulf of Dilmun before catching glimpse of it – much farther south than it had been when he was growing up in the City of Ur.

As he came to the top of the final hill along the Great River, Eber paused and closed his eyes. Bittersweet memories flowed freely. After so long away, he could not have suppressed his emotions if he wanted to. Eber figured people would excuse a man more than 400 years old for being sentimental.

Three weeks earlier, he ascended a ridge overlooking the City of Babylon. Surveying the city now pejoratively called "Babel" by the masses, Eber had been struck most by what was missing.

The Tower, originally called *The Foundation of Heaven On Earth,* now was just a shrinking pile of rubble. Tears streamed down Eber's cheeks as he thought about all that had happened – and how it began with a dream so long ago.

Eber's grandfather, Arpachshad, was born only two years after The Deluge to Noah's son, Shem. "Arpa" was revered by pretty much everyone in his family and community – including the descendants of Noah's other sons, Ham and Japheth. Arpa even got along with his four brothers, most of the time.

Of course, the exception to his amicable circle of comrades had been Nimrod, the wayward son of his cousin. But everyone knew Nimrod only admired himself.

The rift in Eber's family began before he was born, so he learned early to avoid sensitive topics and loud debates. Mostly he preferred to sit in the back and listen. Yet for some annoying reason, he always seemed to end up in the middle of major events. Most significant was a dream that became his nightmare.

Eber thought back to how it all began as he started walking down the path toward the river. To the annoyance of his young assistants, Eber stopped again, and smiled. A gentle wind swirled around him, and he sensed a familiar presence.

"Greetings, my son," the Companion said. "Do you remember the day we met?"

"A Day of Days," Eber replied. "You changed my life."

"What changed most?"

Eber smiled, thought about the Tower, and turned to reply. But the Companion was gone. He had a way of coming and going, yet his presence remained as tangible and comforting today as it was the first time they met so long ago.

Eber stifled a laugh. *What changed? Pretty much everything. Especially me.*

That encounter seemed like it had happened in another lifetime – yet like yesterday. Eber was only 15 years old when he dreamed big and met the Companion. It was a late summer afternoon, and everyone had taken a break from tending the sheep to get out of the sun. Eber laid down in the shade of an oak tree and slowly drifted into his vision of a tower to heaven.

***

Eber found himself walking on a road paved with gold toward a structure rising thousands of feet above the desert floor, with one-story mud brick houses fanning out from it for miles.
The Tower stood out, no doubt.

As the top drifted in and out of lazy Cumulus clouds, his gaze moved down to the huge square foundation. A building that massive took a base wide enough to support it. This one clearly required days to walk all the way around.

Its first level rose hundreds of feet, and then a series of color-coordinated terraces cascaded skyward to a point at the top, ziggurat fashion.

Eber approached the Tower's base and saw large steps leading up to a main level. A man stood waiting at the bottom of the stairs. He was dressed well, albeit modestly – clearly not royalty, but carrying an air of authority Eber could not quite figure out.

"Greetings, Eber," the man said with a gentle smile.

Before Eber could respond, the man motioned for him to go up the stairway. Then he stepped back and leaned on his walking staff. Eber could see the man was done speaking, so he turned and climbed the steps.

At the top, Eber walked through a series of arched tunnels that opened into a three-story covered patio area. Large columns supported the tower around the perimeter of the main lobby. It was bustling, loud, energetic, and fun. There was plenty of music, art, food, and laughter.

Eber also recalled feeling compelled to keep moving. Somehow, he knew he had to get to the top of the Tower, so he worked his way up the building via massive stairs coming off the lobby. As he got higher, the space in each level got smaller and had fewer people. Also, each seemed to have a different purpose – with women spinning yarn, children playing, a man repairing a broken lamp, priests burning incense, couples intimate on a couch, and functionaries writing on clay cuneiform tablets.

Eber kept climbing up a series of narrowing stairwells until he was alone on a terrace with an incredible view of the river valley below. Rising above him was the final piece – the top of the tower, a small three-sided structure pointing toward heaven. Eber knew he still was not done.

Looking closer, he discovered an entrance at the bottom of the building supporting the spire. Inside was a wood ladder leading up to a trap door about 20 feet above him. He ascended the ladder, opened the door, and found himself on a small square piece of wood – with only sky above and a low railing attached to the tiny platform.

For some reason, Eber was not frightened. That alone was a miracle, considering his apprehension of heights, which he called *sensible concern*, not *fear*. As he stood looking up, the air began to stir. A breeze softly swirled around him, enveloped him, and seemed to enter his body and soul – bringing a tangible sense of peace he had never felt before.

A gust of wind blew shut the trap door, with no obvious way to open it from above, but Eber barely noticed. His attention had been drawn skyward.

A glorious light was drifting in and out of the clouds, bright white yet cool to the eyes. Eber was so fixated on the soothing effect of the light he did not notice the wind had lifted him off the roof and was carrying him over the city below.

The longer Eber focused on the light, the more he wanted to fly upward and investigate the source – maybe even meet God face-to-face. But he sensed something was not right.

Eber looked down and saw new details below – thousands of people living in squalor, children starving, fields and vineyards in ruins, dead animals everywhere, extreme violence, injustice, and greed. Fires were burning throughout the city, which appeared to be mostly mounds of rubble. He heard the sound of countless people in pain crying out to God for help.

Then Eber heard a voice above him say: "You will find me among my suffering children."

***

Eber awoke to his oldest brother banging on a bronze plate and calling workers back to their tasks. But the Tower dream was so vivid, its images remained in his mind for hours, forcing Eber to quietly contemplate it the rest of the day. The vision was a profound experience for a 15-year-old to process, so he did not tell anyone about it – especially not his father.

Shelah had strayed from his family's faith years ago. Eventually he would leverage his skill as a sculptor into a lucrative career as a "Priest" for hire, designing statues of "gods" and praying for them to be imbued with divine power.

Eber's father saw other faiths as just another way to give people hope they could have the things *everyone* wants – such as good crop yields, prosperity, and normal flood cycles.

However, Arpa had remained a devout follower of the Creator, so few were surprised they had a major confrontation when his son was 16 and announced he believed the "One-God" view was antiquated and unsophisticated.

Arpa was concerned Shelah was giving up his faith out of simple greed, looking for a chance to profit as a sculptor of false gods. When Arpa challenged the temple system as being corrupt, especially its questionable sexual benefits, his son responded with disdain.

"Where are all the temples and shrines to *your* god, my father?" Shelah asked.

"The Creator has no need for a temple," Arpa replied. "The Living God can be found everywhere, from the lowest valley to the highest mountains, and from the depths of the oceans to the glory between the stars."

His son started laughing. Before Arpa could respond, Shelah said: "People need something *tangible* to worship, father. They want to experience faith with their senses – a god they can caress, honor, and enjoy in a tactile way.

"Your God has no temples because nobody wants to worship a vapor."

Arpa began to talk again, but he knew it was fruitless to continue the conversation much longer. Shelah had turned from God, and all Arpa could do was make sure the next generation knew the Creator – and that meant Eber.

A loud and serious shout to "get back to work" interrupted Eber's thoughts, so he got up, brushed the chaff off his skirt, and followed his brothers out. Shepherding tasks were a welcome diversion the day of his dream. Back then, life was less complicated, though not always as comfortable.

***

By the time Eber was born, 67 years after The Deluge, the hardest work of rebuilding had been done. Also, much of nature had recovered, so Eber grew up in a world of lush plants, abundant wildlife, and mature fields and vineyards.

All of it could have been maintained if humans had spread out after The Deluge, but most disobeyed God and drifted south together, clustering in cities.

At first it seemed as if God, or maybe Noah, had gotten it wrong. Progress jumped out to a fast start when the post-flood population explosion fueled technology innovation, especially in agriculture. Intensive year-round food production was enabled by canals that diverted water to fields and limited damage from floods. In high water, the larger canals even became navigable for boats and were used for trade and communication.

Everything was going great, until they realized building cities had a severe cost.

With little wood or stone natural to the area, they resorted to massive dredging for mud, sand, and reeds to make bricks. It left the Great Marsh a desolate wasteland. Much of the wildlife and flora disappeared before anyone realized there was a problem.

When Eber was a teen-ager, you could still find water buffalo in the marshlands and gazelles in the deserts. Eventually both areas were decimated by construction of the cities and the Tower, but Eber often would go with his brothers to hunt for ducks, partridges, and snipes. Sometimes they would branch from waterfowl and look for small mammals such as badgers, otters, and muskrats.

However, the young Sons of Shelah spent most of their waking hours ensuring the family's sheep and livestock got safely from their sheds to grazing grounds early in the morning, and back again in the afternoon. Those mundane tasks were welcome distractions the day Eber had his dream.

Late that afternoon, he was tasked with herding the flock back to their pens. As he casually walked down the path – at a decent pace because it was almost feeding time for the animals – Eber saw a man approaching in the distance. As he drew close, a warm breeze enveloped them both. Then Eber froze.

It was the man from his dream about the Tower. Instead of recoiling, Eber impulsively ran toward him, slid to a stop just in time, and stared at the man's face while trying to think of the right words to say. He felt a tangible sense of calm, and it was exactly like his feeling in the dream.

Eber had so much he wanted to say that he said nothing.

"Are you alright?" the man asked after a few minutes.

"I'm not sure," Eber said. "I had a very strange dream today and don't know what it means. Also, and I know this will sound ... um, *unusual* ... but you were in my dream."

The man turned to face Eber and looked pensive.

"The meaning of your dream about the Tower will take a lifetime to learn, Eber," he said. "You will have great joy and great sadness along the way. But even in loss, you will never be alone or forsaken."

"How did you know my name?" Eber asked. "And how did you know about my dream?"

"Because I am your Companion. I was there for your first breath, and I will be there for your final breath."

***

Eber started to speak but the sound of footsteps caused him to rotate and see three friends jogging up the path. When he turned back, the man was gone. Eber thought about looking for him, but his friends wanted to get home.

They were late for a family celebration with the Ham side of the family. One of his cousins was turning 12, and Uncle Nimrod always threw the best parties.

Nimrod was larger than life in his prime. A renowned hunter and builder of cities, he had rejected the faith of his fathers by age 18. Nimrod saw God as a tyrant who forced people to be dependent on him through fear, though he later became the gold standard for that model.

He often complained that it made no sense to worship a God who had murdered most of the human race. Usually that was slurred over a mug of beer with his sons, who accompanied their doting father on most hunts and every feast.

The king's obsessive need to build cities drove rapid development in construction tools and techniques, mathematics, and literacy. It also provided new economic opportunities for people, drawing many from rural farms to the cities. Competition for Nimrod's favor among cities and temples became so intense a "bigger is better" mentality arose on an epic scale – including palaces, temples, ziggurats, and many other large urban projects.

The downside, of course, was the death of thousands and destruction of the environment.

Eber could not criticize his relative on the night of the party. At Nimrod events, teen-age boys were allowed to drink wine and beer. As usual, Eber congregated at a large table with his brothers, relatives, and friends – close enough for the girls to see, while keeping up a pretense of indifference as they ate wild boar and told embellished stories. Soon Eber all but forgot his dream.

Everyone was well into dinner when a commotion at the door drew their attention. A small but lavishly attired entourage entered. Eber immediately scanned the room for Arpa, who would not be happy the Priestess of the moon god was attending.

The woman had just returned from dedicating a new temple called "House of Joys" in the northern city of Harran. It was planted as an extension campus by a temple based in Ur named "House of The Great Light," dedicated to the moon god Nanna.

Normally other religions did not bother Eber much, because most temples were just squat mud-brick squares with small congregations. They all talked a lot about expanding, but everyone was just hoping to tap into the steady flow of people returning from the First Sending.

However, the Nanna cult was much more sophisticated than most, and its campaign of "Outcomes That Matter" for young adults was especially successful. It was a clever way of saying you could have anything you want if you believed in Nanna.

Since they worshiped the moon god, they often boasted of Nanna's ability to produce crop prosperity for those who gave of their first fruits loyally. Their most popular item was "Miracle River Water," pulled from the Great River and blessed by the Priestess herself.

When a young man from the Nanna group sat down at Eber's table, he quickly changed the conversation to his pantheon of gods. He kept calling Nanna the "father of gods" and claimed the God of Noah was dead. For a finale, he stood up with a dramatic gesture, spilled beer on his over-tunic, giggled, and boasted about how priests of Nanna had used dreams to predict the future.

Eber impulsively stood up and said, with clear disdain and louder than he intended:

"I had a prophetic dream this afternoon, but it didn't come from the moon."

Eber immediately regretted the sarcastic comment when his table erupted in laughter, jeers, and calls for more beer. He tried talking over the laughter to minimize the damage, explaining it was a tower in the middle of a desert and obviously just a metaphor. Instead of helping, his efforts only evoked a second wave of banter about "The Tower of Eber."

Then the worst thing possible happened: Nimrod walked up to the table.

***

The son of Cush, son of Ham, and grandson of Noah, Nimrod was a huge man with indefatigable energy. At 6-foot-5 and 250 pounds of muscle, he could take over a room by walking in the door. Nimrod loved to hang out with friends, hunt and fish, eat and drink, slap women on their posteriors, and talk about conquests to come.

Nimrod also had a fierce contempt for any serious conversations about religion. When it came to God, Arpa and Nimrod were on opposite shores of the Great Sea. Grandfather said the Creator had given Noah's family a second chance to walk with him like we had in the Garden. Nimrod figured Noah's God had walked away from his creation, so he would return the favor.

Eber paused at the thought of Nimrod. So much had happened since then. But he would always remember Nimrod as he was that day, a virile man who was excited about the future. That is why Eber felt such mixed emotions when Nimrod walked up, leaned over the table full of adoring young men, and said:

"What is so funny at *this* table?"

"Eber had a dream about a tower to heaven," someone blurted out. "Who builds a tower in the desert high enough to reach God?"

That elicited another round of laughter. But Nimrod said nothing, so the table quickly became quiet. He looked at Eber, walked over to his chair, put his arm around his shoulder, leaned in, glanced up at the other people and said:

"That's OK, Eber, I had the same dream. And I will build that tower. But it will not be *for* God. It will be to *spite* him."

Then Nimrod scanned the puzzled faces at the table, broke out in a hearty laugh, and said: "Now enough dreaming! Let's enjoy being awake – at least for as long as we can. Anybody need more beer?"

The crowd collectively roared and changed the subject to the upcoming harvest festivals. Eber did his best to participate but took the first opportunity to slip away early. On his way out the door, a girl appeared out of the shadows, put her hands on her hips, and blocked his path.

"I'd like to hear about your dream," she said, looking serious.

Eber was in no mood to engage Azurad, the precocious 10-year-old daughter of Nimrod, so he mumbled something about needing to help his father and left. About halfway across the courtyard, he looked back and saw Azurad standing in the doorway with her arms crossed. She stared at him with a disapproving look, tightened her belt, turned her back on him, and walked away with purpose.

***

On his way home, Eber pondered how to explain his early exit. But when he entered his family's house, everyone mumbled a collective "hello" and seemed focused on their tasks. Eventually his mother asked how the party went. He told a story that left out key details, figuring nobody was paying attention, but his younger brother picked up on it as Arpa was coming in the door.

"Actually, you got home really early. Any problems?" his brother asked with a mischievous grin.

Eber tried to turn the conversation to the Priestess attending the gala, but that just ramped up family interest – especially from Shelah. Finally, Eber blurted out the story about his dream and the interaction with Nimrod.

At the mention of Nimrod, his father got up from his drawing desk and walked over to the kitchen table.

"He wants to build a tower?" Shelah asked. "Did he say why?"

Eber did not want to go down this rabbit trail, but he saw no other options.

"Only that he would do it someday, and it would be to spite God, not for him," Eber said.

"That must mean he wants to build a new major temple," said Shelah, who looked up at his wife. "My love, that could open the door for our statue business."

Eber was in and out of the rest of the conversation. His father saw it all as a vocational opportunity. His brother wondered how much Eber had to drink. His mother worried it might all be a sign of dark magic from the Night Creatures. His sister wanted to know about *everyone* who was there and what they were wearing. His grandfather just listened silently in a corner chair.

Eventually, the family went to bed one-by-one, until only Eber and Arpa were left. Eber mumbled something about it being a long day, went outside to relieve himself, then returned intending to go to bed. But Arpa was sitting at the kitchen table, and the Companion was standing beside him.

Arpa pointed toward the open chair. Eber sat down – though he never took his eyes off the person his grandfather obviously knew was there but had not yet acknowledged. Arpa leaned forward in his chair, locked eyes with his grandson, and offered what Eber later called his "Three Purposes" teaching:

"Eber, if you remember anything that I teach you, this is most important – God has a purpose for you far beyond your dreams," Arpa said. "He will help you see the world from his point of view.

"In a perfect world, the Garden of Eden, God created human beings for three Great Purposes – to walk with him daily, to have loving relationships with each other, and to be faithful stewards of the world he gave us to tend. We have walked away from all three repeatedly, but God deeply desires for all to be restored.

"That is the most important lesson, my son. We serve a God whose heart is to *restore* his children, and he does it one generation at a time. When it happens, it is a Day of Days."

Eber never forgot that lesson or those three points. He personally fell short of them too often, but his grandfather's teaching had been a compass guiding him back on track throughout life. Of course, Arpa also was inquisitive that night.

"From the sound of it, *today* also was a big day," he said. "I would like to hear more about your tower dream, and that unusual wind."

Then Arpa smiled broadly.

"But first, tell me how you met the Companion."

2

Sole Survivors

A well-worn path directed Eber through the quiet sea village just south of Ur, past its fish market and community gardens, and out to the rural farmland in rolling hills beyond.

A mile down a winding path, he came to the familiar cottage of his grandfather. Eber paused before entering, not certain what to expect after so long away. During his final visit, Arpa was waiting for him in a chair under a makeshift tent made from blankets, playing a game using colored rocks with children more than 400 years younger. It evoked a flood of fond memories, especially of Eber's teen years in Ur.

He put his hand on Arpa's chair and thought how many hours he had spent listening to his grandfather talk about the Creator while sitting in the same place staring at the sea. When he was a child, Eber never could get enough of the stories about Noah, the Ark, and all things Deluge. The tales were always action-packed and rich in detail.

However, Arpa rarely talked about his grandfather, Noah. Eber only met the patriarch once before the Second Sending, and there was little conversation.

Noah was a soft-spoken, introverted farmer who lost his wife too soon after The Deluge. He settled in a modest homestead in the northern highlands – with a vegetable garden, vineyard, a few chickens, sheep, and two cows – until migrating to Canaan to be with his son Shem late in life.

The rebuilding was just starting when Arpa was born in Cizre City two years after The Deluge, so the experience was still fresh for Noah's family. When Eber listened to survivors tell stories about the years before and after The Deluge, one thing came through clearly: Those eight people went through hell on earth and came through on the other side.

And they needed supernatural help to do it.

***

Imagine being almost 400 years old and having God tell you that in 120 years the world will end, you will have produced your first children, and you will build a huge ship to save them from doom. Eber wondered what he would have done with that information. Noah and his wife used it to save their children not yet conceived.

But it was a long and hard mission. Noah and his family worked on the Ark – naming it *The Preserver of Life* – for more than a century. The entire time they warned everyone they could to turn from the rampant violence that had permeated humanity.

Many refused to believe a good God would destroy the world he created. But Noah always said, "God is like any other father – he will tolerate a lot of poor behavior, but when his children started hurting each other he has to step in."

And step in he did. First, God revealed the coming world destruction – and family – to Noah along with instructions for an Ark. That alone was a lot to process, especially for his wife.

Emzara, the granddaughter of Methuselah, was unable to bear children for more than 300 years after marrying Noah. She had given up hope about 200 years earlier, so this prophecy felt like a cruel joke. However, she changed her mind unexpectedly.

A few years into the project, she approached Noah at their inland shipyard and began to complain about how much of their money was going into materials for the Ark. When the conversation became heated, she abruptly left and took a long walk home to cool down. Along the path to their small threshing shed, she had what she called "a brief conversation" with a man who persuaded her to support *The Preserver of Life*.

When probed for details later, Emzara would always break out in a broad smile and begin singing a popular song, "Back To The Garden."

Whatever happened in her interaction with the stranger, Emzara returned a changed woman. She walked in the door, told Noah she believed him, was all-in on building *The Preserver*, had faith God would give them children, and was confident he would save them from the destruction to come.

"God is so good, he warned us a century ahead," Emzara often said when spirits were low. Then she would talk about how the Lord even gave Adam and Eve plenty of advance notice.

"We cannot forget this is about restoration, not punishment," she said. "God wants all people to turn and be saved."

Her choice to support Noah literally saved the human race. Her faith in God's ability to give her a family was even more profound. Within a year she was pregnant. And over the next six years she gave birth to three sons. Arpa said people forget his grandmother was almost 400 years old when she had her first child, so the miracles really started a century before The Deluge.

And that was just the beginning. For more than 100 years, the family took on the time-consuming work of warning all they could while building the Ark. At first, Noah's message resonated. A large faith community arose around the Ark called "The Preservers." Their financial support and connections were critical in getting the materials needed.

But after about 50 years of hard labor, rigid religious practices, and no rain, the crowds started to thin. More and more of the work fell on eight aging men and women. By the time the flood hit, Noah was 600, Japheth 100, Shem 98 and Ham 96.

Also, the project was mammoth. *The Preserver* was 510 feet long, 85 feet wide, and 51 feet high. Made with laminated gopher wood, sealed with bitumen, and covered by a roof overlapping the sides with an 18-inch gap for ventilation, it was water-tight short of a complete roll. They hoped.

Built to be a cargo ship, *The Preserver* had three decks, with multiple rooms throughout each. It had a large attached stationary stern rudder extending from below the keel to about 10 feet above the top deck, where it doubled as a wind stabilizer.

The animals were loaded up a ramp and through a massive door on the side of the middle deck, amidship. Securing that door would be critical for the boat to float.

Were it not for the few remaining Nephilim, the Ark might not have been completed before The Deluge hit. These giants of old had been declared sub-human and were hunted for sport, but a few were hidden and protected by Noah. They repaid his kindness by arriving a week before the Day of Reckoning to set the upper level in place. They also helped to herd the large animals in – reducing a months-long process to a few days.

Family lore said Noah felt sorry for them and hid two with the large animals on the lowest level, but nobody had ever seen one.

***

Thankfully, the Ark's design and construction were high quality – much due to Japheth, who had spent years studying with ship builders and sailors. Those skills were passed down to his descendants, but The Deluge was an historic event. Sailing into unknown waters became a whole different kind of pressure.

The family had no idea what would happen once disaster struck, other than they would be at the mercy of God. He never failed them. Every time they faced a crisis, God did something miraculous to energize the enterprise. Of course, the biggest event was The Deluge itself, which began when God gave Noah seven days to get in the Ark and batten the hatches.

Details captivated Eber from childhood because his Great-Grandfather Shem had *really* lived through it all. Arpa always started the story this way:

"On the Day of Reckoning, the fountains of the Great Deep burst forth and the windows of heaven opened."

First came the earthquakes, which grew in intensity daily. Villages were flattened, trees were knocked down, and large cracks in the earth formed throughout the region. Springs in the area began to boil and smell like rotten eggs.

During one massive quake, all dry dock scaffolding collapsed as *The Preserver* shifted on its keel blocks. Fortunately, they were able to right the ship the next day.

Then the air changed. For millennia, the atmosphere had been a temperate mist that diffused sunlight into placid rainbows of bright colors and sparkles. But in the span of a few weeks, the air had become crystal clear, cool, and dry.

And all the rainbows were gone.

Anvil-shaped Cumulonimbus clouds started building high into the sky, and soon scattered showers developed throughout the area – accompanied by strong wind gusts that seemed to come from every direction. It was the first time the family had ever seen rain.

About an hour into the precipitation, springs began erupting into large geysers more than 500 feet in the air. That hot spray was driven by the wind into the rain showers, blending into deadly storms of scalding water that eradicated entire villages.

At the same time, the earthquakes became so violent it was hard for the family to even stand as they walked up the ramp, grateful they had loaded all animals, gear, and food earlier. Then they watched in horror as mountains to the east began to crumble and large fissures opened in the valley floor below, releasing a river of boiling water that completely engulfed the nearby town.

The family hurried inside, but when they tried to close the 500-pound side door with ropes, it was too heavy to lift without the pully systems on the scaffolding – now in a heap on the rocks below. Shem and Ham scrambled to construct a makeshift replacement but were driven back inside and behind a flood door by the super-heated rain.

Things looked bleak. If the door remained open, *The Preserver* would quickly fill with water and sink, and they would drown. All the workers had evacuated to nearby caves for shelter, so nobody could help the family now. That led to one of Eber's favorite stories – how God himself closed the door of the Ark.

The tipping point came when a massive earthquake caused an avalanche of rocks that ended up resting against *The Preserver's* starboard side. Next, the wind began to blow from the east and build in strength by the minute. Noah's sons decided to make a final attempt to close the door, but a massive storm was raging with hurricane-force winds, torrential rain, lightning, thunder, and funnel clouds. The family huddled together behind the flood door and began praying loudly to God for help, out of options and hope.

Without warning, the roaring of the wind stopped completely – a thunderous noise replaced by an eerie silence among the 70,000 animals and eight humans.

That was followed by what the family described as warm, gentle, and reassuring breeze that wafted through the ship.

Then they heard footsteps outside approaching the Ark. Someone walked up the ramp, pushed the door closed firmly, latched it, then walked away. Just as quickly, the quiet was replaced by the return of the maelstrom.

The family had little time to contemplate what had just happened. Immediately there was an arduous amount work to do. But the fear was gone, so they all got up to do tasks – singing songs of thanksgiving as they walked through *The Preserver*. The music had an incredible calming effect on humans and animals. At least for one night.

Unfortunately, that was just the start. It would be a year before they saw land or sunlight again. For 40 days and 40 nights, the heavy rain was relentless. About a week into The Deluge, the Ark's bow began to rise. Japheth was concerned about the rocks resting against its sides, but the following day the entire craft shifted to a level position in rising water, then began to bob on the surface and float freely. The next time they walked on land, nothing would be the same.

After 40 days, the torrential downpour settled into a light rain, but *The Preserver* was still pummeled by gale-force wind and large waves for another three months. No living creature got much sleep, and it was hard to tell day from night without much light beyond candles and lamps. Ark life then settled into seven more months of monotonous, pain-staking work while continually being buffeted by swells, wind gusts, fear over what to expect, and grief too painful to process yet.

Their sorrow was unfathomable. Eber often wondered how those eight people were able to cope with losing so much – every member of the women's families, businesses and friendships they had built over decades, homes and farms they had constructed from nothing, and now the loss of any certainty in their future. All they could do was focus on tasks and trust God for the rest.

Fortunately, they had a good God and a good mix of skills.

***

Though Noah was a farmer at heart, he became an expert in construction and management. During their time on the Ark, he filled in when people were hurt or sick. Emzara was an animal lover her entire life and knew more about their care than anyone. Also, her faith carried the younger women emotionally during the darkest days of The Deluge.

Japheth had become a master ship builder, and in the process learned how to work with metal and wood, so he could forge daggers, spears, and shields. His wife, 'Adataneses, or "Aunt Ada," was a teacher who knew how to read and write in cuneiform. Her understanding of arithmetic helped in making design calculations.

Shem loved the land and became an expert in agriculture, like his father. He ensured the Ark had ample food stores. Shem also worked with his wife, Sedeqetelebab, on recipes that efficiently matched meal planning with crop production. In addition, her knowledge of herbal medicines was critical in the new world.

Ham was all about animals. He diligently performed chores caring for the livestock and sheep, but he relished working with the Wilds most. He later leveraged that understanding into becoming a master hunter. His wife, Na'eltama'uk, had a special love for horses, though she lovingly tended all the animals.

When others were especially down, she would ride a stallion though the Ark singing war songs until everyone was laughing to the point of tears.

Still, that year in the Ark felt like an eternity.

***

Eventually, *The Preserver* ran aground, which was both a relief and concern as they anxiously waited for the floodwaters to recede enough to depart the ship. Though they longed to be on solid ground, they had no idea what it would look like. After three months, they spotted the tops of nearby mountains. At least they knew the waters were draining and they were not sitting on the highest peak.

Noah wanted to learn if there was widespread dry ground, so he released a raven from the top deck. It just flew circles over the Ark for a while and returned. Then he sent out a dove, but it came back empty-handed. That seriously dashed the family's hopes of a quick resolution. Seven days later, Noah sent out another dove. That one returned with an olive branch, which was a much-needed gift of optimism. After seven more days, Noah sent out yet another dove.

When it did not return, the family knew the bird had found safe ground. They were less certain about their own safety, so they fussed over preparations for three days before opening the door. Finally, Noah's wife broke the ice.

"Well, we could always just spend the rest of our lives stuck on this boat," Emzara said, "but I vote we take a look."

The family laughed in unison, then went to the weather deck – a raised platform on the upper level – and removed its covering to look for dry ground. They saw much more. A gloriously restored world extended out in a panoramic vista, with blue skies, mountains all around, and a large fertile valley to the south.

Though they had landed on the side of a mountain, in God's providence the first season was summer. Most uplifting, they soaked in their first sunlight in more than a year. The beautiful weather was a much-needed morale boost, so they opened the side door, dropped the ramp, and walked down to rocky land – humanity's sole survivors.

Their first act was to build a small altar out of rocks, gather some wood for a fire, then sacrifice and burn a few animals and birds to God as a thanksgiving offering. After what the family had been through on that ship, they were just grateful to be alive and finally have some hope.

The impulsive and genuine act of gratitude, which had been expressed in a blood offering, clearly pleased God. He rewarded the family with a promise not to destroy the earth by flood again – sealing the agreement by restoring rainbows as a reminder.

"That's why any time we feel overwhelmed, we look to the rainbow and remember God's Promise," Arpa often said. "He has restored all things before, and he will do it again."

Though true, the day of the Promise was bittersweet for the family. They felt relief at being saved, yet sadness for all that had been lost. Noah often said God preserved them to restore the three "Great Purposes of The Garden."

"Now all we have to do is love each other, care for our world, and walk with the Creator every day."

***

And walk they did. The journey out of the high mountains was long and perilous, but it could have been worse. *The Preserver* came to rest between twin peaks in the Ararat Mountains – not on their summits – so they were able to avoid crevasses while working down scree fields and ridge lines heading south. The family decided to release the animals first, figuring some would instinctively find routes off the mountain. They did, and it was amazing to watch.

First, the animals came off the Ark in family units, with no rushing or jostling. That alone was a miraculous site. Once off *The Preserver*, the animals seemed to melt into the rugged terrain, leaving a clear trail for the family to follow. Still, just unloading all the creatures and gear took several weeks.

The Ark had settled at about 13,000 feet, so the hike down was slow and difficult at times. The family had to descend steep trails cut by floodwaters that were still draining while dragging supplies on make-shift carts. Atop *The Preserver*, they had spotted Van Lake to the southwest and figured their best option was to head there and get out of the high mountains.

After weeks of cautiously descending rocky trails marked only by tracks left by the animals, they came to the lake. Its water was too salty to drink, but the lake was fed by multiple freshwater streams with abundant fish, so they set up a camp while they scouted. Then came the second part of God's Promise – seasons.

***

Temperatures began to drop daily, eventually bringing light snow, so the family settled into makeshift huts on the southeast shore of Van Lake. Though they were at almost 5,400-foot elevation, that first winter was short and mild. Still, at the first break in weather they scouted how to get to lower elevations.

The lake had no outlet to follow downstream, and terrain was too steep on three sides in or out, so the family broke camp and headed the only direction they could – southeast. Eventually they came to Lake Umia, another saltwater lake with no outlet but with 13 rivers and many small springs feeding it.

At this altitude, about 4,000 foot, the terrain was much less challenging, so their feelings of constant anxiety began to wane. They also had abundant wildlife and wild wheat now. Noah and his family finally could rest, repair, and scout.

During that summer Noah and his sons made two trips back to the Ark, bringing down essential items such as seeds, tools, and clothing. The following year they were able to make one trip, but *The Preserver* already was half covered by snow and ice. That was the last time they saw it.

The breakthrough in their descent came when Shem discovered the Arrow River. The family realized it had found a water highway to lower elevations and, eventually, an ocean. When Ham scouted west and found the Great River, they deduced the Land Between had rich possibilities. When Japheth took expeditions further west and east, they also found access to the sea with its fishing and trade potential.

Despite the possibilities, survival was the highest priority in a world of unknown threats. Since there was safety in numbers, the three brothers and their families lived within a few miles of each other in the northern highlands for the first 25 years. They focused on having children and establishing secure homesteads.

When Arpa talked about those years, he would choke up with emotion. "My Grandmother said those years we learned God wasn't just *with* us, he was *for* us – all the time."

Their biggest challenge came when Emzara died peacefully in her sleep with husband Noah at her side, the night before the 25th anniversary of The Deluge. Soon after her burial, Noah gathered his family and laid out what God wanted in the First Sending.

The message was simple: For your own good, spread out and do not all gather in one spot. Bunching together had been disastrous the first time, so kicking off the new world without having to deal with urban problems seemed sensible anyway.

When the families fanned out from Noah in different directions, most of Shem's tribe went south, including Eber's grandfather. It was the last time Arpa saw his uncle Ham, though many of his cousins came to Babylon for a service when he died.

Eber paused at the memory. It made him think of the frail old man who used to nap in the empty chair next to him, and a deep sadness came over him.

Then he felt the comforting presence of the Companion, standing beside him in silence. Eber exhaled deeply, and the two stood together watching the sea until evening.

3

Divided Families

When Eber was in Ur, he would rise before dawn, walk down a hill to a ridge overlooking the Gulf, pull a lute from his rucksack, sit on a wood bench, and play for God. His day always seemed to flow better when he could start with that perspective.

Eber attributed it to being from a creative family. Women tended to be musicians and men were artisans – potters, jewelers, metal smiths, stone masons, carpenters, and other crafts. Though music became his lifelong hobby, for a vocation Eber preferred commerce, and he had a special knack for international trade.

As much as he hated to admit it, Eber got his business savvy from his father. Shelah started off as a world-class engraver and sculptor. At age 21, he designed a statue of a huge warrior-god wearing a helmet with large horns coming from each side. That piece caught the eye of a key official at the Temple of Enlil – the local god of earth, wind, air, and storms.

The temple's High Priest felt it captured much of what they envisioned Enlil looking like, and they wondered if he would do a custom version for their new hall.

It was Shelah's big break. Enlil was the patron god of Nippur City and direct son of Anu, "god of gods," so his statue was placed prominently in the main hall of their temple, "The Mountain House." That contract led to projects with other temples in the ever-growing pantheon, beginning with the goddess considered Enlil's mother and Anu's consort, Ninhursag, the "Lady of the Sacred Mountain." Just going through major deities brought in enough business to last the family for years.

Eventually, delivering a statue was just the beginning of Shelah's revenue stream. The custom was for an idol-maker to bless a statue, thereby giving it specific powers. After that, he would provide maintenance on a regular basis, offering sacrifices and re-infusing a god's powers – for additional fees, of course.

In the case of the "Twelve Gods of Babylon," that was a monthly ritual.

All the "priest" had to do was place his hands on the statues, loudly pray for them to have the attributes people wanted, and then collect his fee. Requests ranged from productive harvests and seasonal rains to wisdom and justice.

Soon it became much more work than Shelah could handle himself, so he brought on family members as assistants in the business – starting with a nephew, Nahor. The family jumped into the windfall wholeheartedly, with one exception. Nahor's grandson Abram refused to be involved.

***

Abram always seemed to be a little different from the rest of his family. Eber was more than 200 years older, but the two connected immediately because they had so much in common. Both were from the City of Ur, were Shemites, believed in the Living God, hated idolatry, yet had fathers who worked as polytheistic priests.

While growing up, both Eber and Abram had been forced to sit in on complex and aimless debates about gods and demons. During those interactions, Eber often came away more confused than enlightened. All gods seemed equal, except for the god of the person talking at the moment.

Arpa said real truth was simple, so Eber tried to boil it down. He started with who each god *was*, as well as what they could *do*. He rationalized a real god would stand out in the crowd. And if one of the gods truly was a "creator" god, then that god's very nature would be different from all the others – the only un-created living thing in the universe.

Most of Shelah's friends saw the Creator as just one of many gods in an ever-growing storyverse with endless possibilities for income. Eber saw God as being much bigger – one seen more clearly in the stars than in statues.

Soon after he turned 12, Eber finally took a stand on the issue with his father. Shelah brought him into his studio one afternoon to show off his newest work. It was his first small-scale representation of the goddess Ishtar, "Queen of Heaven" and daughter of chief god Anu. The female statuette was nude, adorned only with jewelry made of precious stones and a gold-plated headdress.

"What do you think of the goddess of love and beauty, Eber?" Shelah asked.

Eber scanned the figurine from head to toe, turned to his father, and said, "All I see is a stone statue of a naked lady."

Shelah became visibly angry. "It's not about what you or I believe, but rather about what *other* people believe," he said. "If they believe their god or goddess causes them to be healed or have twelve sons, why should I judge it? Everyone needs hope."

"Even if that is false hope in a false god?" Eber asked.

"Who is to say what is a god and what isn't?" Shelah said. "Besides, believing in only one god is narrow-minded and judgmental these days, my son."

"Even if it is true?" Eber asked.

"Who defines what is true?" Shelah said.

Eber started to reply, but he paused, shook his head, and looked out the window. Even at that age he knew there was no point in continuing. It was especially difficult because it involved the ethics of his father's very lucrative and prestigious career.

Shelah would never change his view and ever change his excuses. Besides, there were many priests and idol-makers in their family, so Eber just listened in silence from that point on as Shelah tried to minimize and justify his practices. However, Eber felt his father was just preying on the fears and superstitions of desperate people.

Eber wanted a real God who was genuine and transcendent. This representation of Ishtar was neither.

Despite that, Shelah's lecture had gone one for five minutes without an apparent breath when Eber's mother entered the room, ascertained the situation, and offered lunch as a way out of their conversation. Eber and his father gratefully changed the subject and never discussed it again.

Their worlds grew further apart when Eber followed the women of the family, taking up music instead of art. His grandmother and mother were both singers who could mesmerize an audience. Unfortunately, he rarely saw his mother sing. She was so in-demand at the temple Main Stage by the time he was a teen-ager that Eber infrequently saw her, from the balcony seats.

Eber had a front-row seat to see his grandmother. Often, she would make up short songs and sing them joyfully while doing chores throughout the home – especially songs thanking God for her family.

For Rasu'aya, performing in public was just practice for her family living room concerts. "Grandmother Rasu" was the first to recognize Eber had a love for music and an aptitude for stringed instruments when he was a child, so she bought him a lute and found someone to teach him.

That gift brought Eber a lifetime of joy. This morning it made him miss his grandmother, so Eber returned from his walk, sat in her chair overlooking the sea, and played her favorite folk song about young love. At the end, Eber felt a wave of melancholy wash over him. His grandmother had died soon after the Tower fell, yet he still missed her very much.

Eber looked at the sky, raised his arms, and thanked God for giving his family such strong women. His grandfather had made that point firmly, and often. In fact, Arpa's strongest memory of the First Sending had been watching his grandmother, mother, and aunts embrace and weep loudly before separating.

The "Women of the Deluge" developed a remarkable bond during their yearlong life-and-death struggle aboard the Ark, and in the hard years before and after the flood. All had lost children to miscarriages along the way, so they shared sorrow and found much-needed comfort in community. Also, living in such close proximity, they had cycled at the same time for decades – spending a week each month together in a tent isolated outside the main camp.

The women came to look forward to their all-female quarantines, if nothing else for conversation about something besides hunting and the weather. Emzara often led the banter and raised the morale of the younger women, so her loss deeply affected them, as if a piece of each had died.

The entire family wept for weeks.

***

Emzara's death devasted Ham, Noah's youngest son, who had developed a close relationship with his mother. Losing her left Ham angry at the world and God, so he lashed out at everyone. It came to a head when he embarrassed his father and paid dearly.

Noah was so distraught over his wife's death, one night he drank too much wine and passed out on his bed with no clothes on. Normally his wife would have been there to cover him. But with Emzara gone, Ham burst into the tent inebriated and hostile, saw his father naked and buttocks-up, laughed in scorn and left in disgust.

When Ham told his brothers, neither laughed. They were mortified by his lack of respect.

Japheth and Shem put a large cloak over their shoulders outside the entrance to Noah's tent, turned to face away from the door, entered walking backward so they would not see their father in that humiliating position, dropped the robe to cover him up without turning around, and left the same way they had entered.

When a servant later told Noah what had happened, he cursed the youngest son of his youngest son. That misfortune fell on Canaan, and it turned out to be a mess Eber did not have to deal with until late in life.

Nobody much trusted Ham after that. Instead of being embarrassed, he just wanted to run away – and said so often. With the First Sending, he was able do just that. He even had a destination, and he didn't care if it was a list of locations pulled by lot out of a wool hat.

Ham wasted no time moving. He said some terse good-byes, loaded his family on carts, headed west toward the Great Sea, then followed its coast south to the Nile River, where many migrated upstream into Egypt and beyond. Ham's entire family left with him, with one notable exception – his grandson, Nimrod.

At first Arpa felt sorry for his cousin being left behind, figuring he had good reasons for the chip on his shoulder. After all, the rest of Ham's family had dark skin and continually reminded Nimrod he was not. His father's name, Cush, means "black." Cush's mother and wife were beautiful dark-skinned women. They also had three handsome black sons. Then Nimrod showed up, and nobody could quite figure out his ethnicity.

Cush's wife was less than enthused when she had to pick up the care of a boy obviously not hers, but she was a godly and compassionate woman who tried to treat him like her own. Her sons did not. Nimrod was continually the object of their jokes and hazing, especially when away from the camp. He was excluded from any significant events and instead was assigned to watch sheep, which he found painfully boring.

Nimrod was never going to fit in or get a break, and the whole family knew it. Cush solved the problem by simply leaving Nimrod behind in the First Sending. But before they moved, his wife had pity on the young man and reached out to Arpa, who was heading to Ur. The family agreed the best solution was for Nimrod to join Shelah's family, but it did not go as planned.

Ham's family left the very next morning, and Nimrod ended up living with them for more than a year. Still, Shelah made efforts to build a relationship with his cousin, taking him hunting soon after he moved in. It was immediately obvious Nimrod was a prodigy – with field skills honed from years of fighting off lions and bears while guarding sheep.

Nimrod was big, strong, fast, instinctual, and relentless. He would be on the trail before anyone else had breakfast, and he would walk in with a gazelle over his shoulders while everyone else was on their second pigeon. Nimrod was so skilled at anticipating animal movements that Shelah decided to send him to relatives in the north highlands, where legendary mountain hunters could mentor him.

Though most hunters killed for meat, Nimrod was driven by the hunt itself – a struggle between man and beast, with only one coming out alive. He compared it to his battle with God, saying he would storm the gates of heaven and take it by force one day. Nobody took him seriously until later.

When Nimrod returned to Ur, he already was famous among the younger generations clustering in the south. Ironically, in his youth Nimrod had been zealous for God. He would only kill animals to sacrifice them to the Lord.

All that changed when he was 18 and a skirmish broke out between his extended family in the north and some militant descendants of Japheth.

***

After learning his family had been attacked and lost key land, Nimrod gathered his hunting buddies into a small Cushite militia, traveled to the site, and defeated the Japhethites. His relatives were so grateful they voted to make him king of the area. That changed everything because he liked it – a *lot*.

Nimrod began to envision his own kingdom and quickly moved away from any interest in the kingdom of God. His fame and pride seemed to grow daily, which of course led to his fall. And the Tower's.

Eber often wondered if Arpa had been jealous of his cousin's celebrity, but his grandfather always seemed content to live a middle way – a lifestyle of moderation outside the cities Nimrod craved. Eber realized he was becoming more like his grandfather each year, but then Arpa had been far more involved in his life than his father.

When Eber launched his first trading network, Arpa had counseled him to focus on barley. It could handle the coming higher salinity of the soil in the south better than wheat, he said. It also could be sold for multiple use cases – breads, soups, stews, brewing, and more. It was great advice. Barley now was equal to silver as a currency, and Eber could live comfortably.

Arpa also taught Eber not to burn bridges, and he modeled it with Nimrod. Arpa showed up when invited, was engaging and respectful, and was savvy enough to leave early so Nimrod's rowdy friends could have their moments of debauchery.

However, any meaningful interaction between Arpa and Nimrod was almost always done without Shelah in the room. Arpa hated the fact his son had a bad case of hero worship when it came to Nimrod, who had been throwing him major business.

After Shelah was named the first Minister of Faiths by Nimrod, he spent most of his time on the road servicing the larger temples. When Eber needed his father most, he was out talking to statues instead of helping his son. The worst was when Eber's mother fell sick and died. He was only 13 years old and reached out to his father, but her loss caused Shelah to withdraw even more – masking his grief by working yet longer hours in his shop.

***

With his father mostly absent, Eber spent even more time with his grandparents. Late in life, Eber saw that as a blessing. He preferred Arpa's prudent approach and love for the land. Plus, his grandmother encouraged his passion for music and was a fabulous cook. His days at the cottage by the Gulf were quiet and peaceful.

Then Nimrod returned from the north, hyping a vision for rebuilding an ancient city south of Ur with a ziggurat temple that would revitalize the area. He met with the family elders and pitched the project.

Shelah was enamored yet again and jumped in immediately, even helping to design the initial seals of Eridu City. Eber had an excuse to avoid involvement. He was needed on the farm with his father gone, so he was released from making a tough choice.

Arpa deferred politely, saying his business took so much time he could not be involved at the moment but would consider it in the future, thank you. His decision to keep the communication lines open with Nimrod led to the most significant family meeting Eber ever attended.

***

One late summer day, Eber and other workers were finishing repairs on a goat pen when Arpa approached. He told Eber to clean up, change clothes, and be ready to head into Ur to the palace within the hour. Then he turned around and walked back to the cottage. Eber knew something unusual was happening, so he complied and was at the gate 30 minutes early.

His grandfather was waiting.

Though Eber had seen the mini-palace Nimrod built on the west banks of the Great River in Ur, he had never been inside until that day. Later in life he could laugh at how unsophisticated he was at age 20, but back then everything seemed oversized, from the glazed burnt-brick walls and columns to the bronze decorations and red curtains with fringes.

Arpa and Eber followed a squad of men wearing bronze armor and carrying spears into a large room. Nimrod was seated on a huge chair on a raised platform at the front.

"Welcome, cousin!" he shouted. "A Day of Days, eh?"

Arpa smiled. Then he graciously greeted Nimrod and his family – each by name – and thanked them for inviting him. Eber was distracted by the luxurious interior, including extensive gold, silver, bronze, and copper decorations throughout. He also noticed one family member was missing, but the conversation pulled his attention back.

The older men and women of the family were discussing terms of an arranged marriage between members of the Shem and Ham families. All were dressed in their finest bright-colored attire, with more silk than Eber had ever seen in one room. The women felt it was a good match. Nimrod and Arpa, both in royal clothes, talked about how the man was now in position to support a family, and she was of age to provide sons. Nimrod's wife mentioned their mutual love for music and curiosity about the God of Noah.

The next words froze in time:

"Eber and Azurad will be perfect together."

What? Me? And who? Eber was still processing the fact he apparently would have to marry a petulant little girl when Nimrod called out, "Azurad!"

***

Around the corner came three young women laughing arm-in-arm. They were dressed for hunting waterfowl, and one had a falcon on her arm. The beautiful young woman in the middle looked oddly familiar to Eber. Her close-fit leather tunic obviously had been designed not to catch on branches in a thicket, and a bow and quiver were slung over her shoulder.

Suddenly, she stopped and scanned the room. Eber realized it was Azurad, and the look on her face indicated she was quickly apprehending the meeting's real agenda.

At least I wasn't the only one left in the dark, he thought.

Eber would have laughed at the obvious communication failure, but he was completely enamored by Azurad's transformation. At 15, she carried herself with more confidence and maturity than her 20-year-old future husband.

Azurad had long red hair that cascaded down her shoulders. Unlike most of her friends, she wore little jewelry – only a single pair of blue earrings – saying it was a bother when working with the animals. But she always wore a headband with a large feather pointing down, usually blue to match her eyes.

Right now, those eyes were getting wider by the moment. Eber could tell Azurad's mind was racing to the uncomfortable conclusion that she had seriously miscalculated the event's true purpose, and that everyone was staring at her in silence.

Finally, she looked at Eber and blurted out, "Oh God."

He smiled and said, "No, I'm just Eber."

Everyone began to laugh, including Azurad, who visibly relaxed. Then Azurad looked up at Nimrod and said, "If I had known what this meeting was about, my father, I would have been in a royal dress."

"But that would have taken all the fun out of it, daughter" Nimrod said with a hearty laugh. "Besides, if I had given you warning, you might have run away."

Azurad slowly turned to face Eber, scanned him from head to toe, bowed respectfully, turned back to her father, and said, "No, I think I will keep this one, my lord."

Nimrod jumped to his feet, laughed loudly, bounded off the platform, wrapped his arms around his only daughter, and embraced her warmly. Then he put her down, looked into her eyes and said, "I bless you and pledge to protect you and your new family. Go in peace."

The betrothed couple was quickly surrounded by family and friends – with loud talking, much joy, and more information about covenant requirements than they could process. Through the commotion, Eber kept looking at Azurad across the room, and she kept looking at him.

When it came to marriage, Azurad and Eber had figured it would end up a business arrangement. Neither expected their attraction – mutual respect, affection, and passion that endured for more than 200 years.

Eber tried to process Azurad's evolution from pesky brat to woman, but the fact he would have the responsibility of a wife kept invading his mind. He was seriously overloaded with a blend of excitement, confusion, anticipation, and terror.

The next few months were a blur to Eber. Everyone told him he was in control of the wedding and marriage, but he knew better. He felt like captain of a ship being towed along – with his hands on the wheel but not really steering it. One day he got frustrated and asked Arpa what to do. His grandfather laughed.

"Just say, 'Whatever you want, my love,' and all will be fine," Arpa said.

***

It was the best advice on marriage Eber ever got. The second-best counsel also came from his grandfather, and it concerned the custom that a marriage did not become legal until the groom delivered a bridal gift to her father.

"What can I afford to offer Nimrod as a gift?" he asked Arpa. "Grandfather, is there anything I can give him that he doesn't already have? This is an impossible task."

Arpa thought for a moment, broke out in a broad smile, and said, "Let me take care of that, Eber."

His grandfather went inside for a few minutes, talked with Rasu, then came back out with his walking stick and a small backpack. He kissed his smiling wife good-bye and left for a week. Arpa returned with a gift that became family legend – a full-length polished bronze mirror in a wood frame, with gold inlays and carvings of hunting scenes throughout.

"What on earth made you think of that?" Eber asked.

"There is only one thing Nimrod truly loves – himself," Arpa said. "Now he can worship what he adores most every day."

Eber and his grandparents laughed for a long time, and then sent a servant to set up a meeting with Nimrod. The king loved getting gifts, so word came back it would happen the next day. As they walked into his throne room, Nimrod was waiting expectantly – with Azurad dressed like a princess.

When Arpa and Eber presented the mirror, Nimrod was ecstatic – posing numerous ways and nodding in approval. He finally turned and said, "Welcome to the family, Eber!"

The bride-to-be and her best friend were laughing so hard they were almost in tears. Finally, Azurad willed herself to stand up, wipe her face, adjust her dress, and appear to be an adult. Then she looked directly at Eber, nodded her head, and tried to suppress a laugh.

***

Their wedding was a joyous occasion at the Nimrod home, with music, food, dancing, and plenty of wine. Eventually Eber and Azurad made the traditional walk to the honeymoon cottage, used by all newlyweds in the village. Adrenaline was still rushing through both from the sheer energy of the event, and they were so focused on their conversation they did not notice a man approaching on the path.

"Greetings, husband and wife!" the man called out cheerfully.

Eber and Azurad paused to thank him, then stopped in their tracks. Eber realized it was the Companion, and that Azurad obviously saw him, too. Azurad recognized this was the man from Eber's dream and was dumbstruck.

The Companion smiled and said: "God's blessing is on you, Eber and Azurad. You will go through much sorrow together, but the Lord himself will help you prevail. In the end, the Sons of Noah will become the Sons of Eber."

Instinctively Eber and Azurad looked at each other in disbelief. When they turned back, he was gone.

"Did you *see* that?" Eber asked.

"Yes! And did you *hear* that?" Azurad replied.

"Sons of *who*?" he asked.

"Apparently sons of *you*," she said. "So that better mean sons of *me*!"

They looked at each other, started laughing, then crying, then embracing, and then kissing as lovers.

Eber had to interrupt the memory, because soon he would be sobbing. That moment and that night, Azurad had become more than his wife. She became his life partner and great love, and he missed her more than he could permit himself to admit.

4

Rise of Nimrod

The aroma of freshly baked date bread greeted Eber as he returned from a morning walk to the Gulf overlook, triggering sweet memories of breakfast at his grandmother's house years earlier.

"Nobody leaves my home hungry, unloved, or empty-handed," Rasu often said. She meant it. Breakfast was a feast of warm breads, figs and pomegranates, cheeses, yogurt, and goat milk. And before you left, Rasu would hand you a roll of fruit and cheese wrapped in flatbread for the day.

Eber walked outside and saw the herb garden his grandmother had toiled to keep up for decades. His mind flashed to an image of his two favorite women in the same spot years earlier – on their knees, weeding and pruning, and joyfully gossiping about family.

Azurad and Rasu had bonded immediately. They shared a love of the outdoors, hospitality, thoughtful conversations, music, and especially the children. Eber paused and smiled. Azurad often said she saw God most in her grandchildren.

His wife had her own deep faith, inspired by her grandmother, Na'eltama'uk, wife of Ham. While Azurad's father and brothers would be out hunting with the men, she would spend long hours riding on horses with "Grandmother Na'el" and listening to stories about how God had helped the family through difficult years.

Shared oral history became a strong connecting point for Eber and Azurad – and later for their children. But their marriage brought together more than two people. It reunited Noah's family, for better and for worse.

Unfortunately, the peace was short-lived.

Deep divisions in the family had started when Ham embarrassed Noah. It had been carried on by Cush and his brothers, so it took only one major spark to relight the fire. That came when Nimrod returned from the north and announced a plan to rebuild Eridu City south of Ur. Its showcase was to be a new temple to Enki, the city's patron god who represented deep waters, wisdom, magic, and more.

The news shook Eber out of a complacency that had developed over years of only hearing about Nimrod's exploits from afar. He had learned to tolerate the stories of his father-in-law's grand hunts, ribald parties, and audacious development aspirations in the north. Even when Nimrod formed an alliance headquartered in Babylon with Arpa's brother Ashur, it seemed too far away to be a problem.

However, Nimrod's plan to build up Eridu, and later Babylon, would bring his influence too close to home for Eber. Those projects would attract large numbers of people and create huge challenges. Based on history, this was not going to end well.

Worse, at the Eridu banquet Nimrod stood at a podium telling the descendants of Noah to ignore the aging founders of the New World and listen to the emerging next-generation culture. Eber cringed as he recalled the lavish Eridu event, starting with a banner above the head table that blared "Generation of Secession: This Changes Everything."

A committee of "Religious Progressives" coined the phrase as an in-your-face statement to the Creator. They believed God had no right to pick heaven all for himself, leaving only the "lower world" to humans, so they advocated building a tower with an idol on top holding a sword. The point was simple: Humans could run the universe better than God had, so it was time for a change.

Also, secession meant more than overthrowing God from his throne in heaven. Adherents believed God had done a terrible job of managing humans and the earth, so it was time for a "progressive transformation" from reliance on a judgmental deity to communities fueled by human ingenuity. That revolt would be led by a new generation of leaders, the "Generation of Secession."

Initially people debated how to overpower heaven with force, but the more serious threat ended up being a passive-aggressive strategy that caught Nimrod's eye.

The "Rainbow Promise Movement" claimed God had completely and eternally forgiven all sins after The Deluge. In their statement of faith, the Rainbow Promise offered a three-point platform:

- God felt guilty about killing most humans,
- God now knew humans would always come up short,
- So God no longer would condemn human behavior.

Translation: Everybody gets into heaven, no matter what they do. Eber figured the movement really was just an excuse for people to do things that were repugnant in general, not just to God. Besides, forgiveness had come only a blood sacrifice.

The atonement offering appeased God temporarily, but he wanted their obedience more than their sacrifices. Unfortunately, that kind of personal responsibility never caught on with the public, so the Rainbow Promise movement ended up wildly popular. Nimrod noticed, and later he used it to solve a major problem at the Tower.

***

Halfway through construction, workers started leaving the project – many to avoid starvation, death from disease, or one of the frequent on-site accidents. Leaders did not seem to care. They were less concerned with safety than quotas and deadlines, so they simply broadened their net and recruited replacement workers from outside the area. However, those workers brought in different languages, customs, and religions – and soon they demanded their gods have equal standing.

In a brilliant marketing move, Nimrod launched a campaign called "The Year of Tolerance" to keep disgruntled workers happy. The idea of everyone getting into heaven was a messaging masterstroke. Faith leaders applauded it as a step toward cultural relevance in a pluralistic society. However, one of the campaign tenets was to ban the use of the term "Living God" as discriminatory against other gods.

Yes, we will tolerate every god – except for the only real one, Eber thought.

Nimrod consistently reinforced the message, down to ending every speech by having the crowd raise a fist and shout: "Tolerance over Judgment!"

Arpa said it was "tolerance over justice." Still, the city's campaign of acceptance without accountability was received with enthusiasm. Eventually the people of Babylon elevated tolerance over truth itself. And in the end, Nimrod did not have to conquer Babylonia. The people *asked* him to be king.

"We take the first step toward our future today," a speaker said, drawing Eber's attention back to the Eridu announcement. "Cities spark new ideas, yet the God of Noah would reserve creativity for himself. We say, no longer. Please welcome the visionary who will lead us there, our king, Lord Nimrod!"

The crowd roared in approval as Nimrod strolled to the front waving, clearly basking in the attention of being newly minted royalty. After laying out his master plan for a city and surrounding food production centers, Nimrod thanked investors – offering special praise to the Enki organization for its generous contributions to the community, saying they had far outbid other faiths for the Central City location.

But nothing about Eridu City felt right to Eber. First, naming a building at the edge of a festering swamp "House of the

Deep Waters" seemed odd even for Nimrod. Stranger was the fact that people immersed themselves in its rancid water to be "cleansed."

Second, Eber was concerned about the potential impact of large agricultural complexes on local farmers who owned fields southeast of Ur, in the green belt between the cities.

Third, he believed the construction and influx of laborers would harm the area's environment, so he was barely listening to friends when Nimrod approached during the post-event wine and cheese party and said:

"Eber, are you interested in joining our enterprise?"

Eber was completely unprepared to confront the issues here and now, and no answer running through his mind seemed safe or appropriate. Fortunately, his new wife came to the rescue.

Azurad stepped between the two and said: "Father, not *yet*, please. We just got married and need some time to work on giving you grandchildren ... if you know what I mean."

The princess put her hands on her hips, and her face broke into a mischievous grin. Nimrod chuckled, clapped his hands, and said loudly: "Yes! Go be fruitful and multiply, daughter!"

In the ensuing revelry, Arpa skillfully led Eber and Azurad out of the room – and eventually out of Nimrod's inner circle.

***

Over the next 50 years, they saw Azurad's side of the family less and less. Most were engaged in the Eridu projects, and later the City of Babylon.

Azurad and Eber focused on building their family and a business in grain trading that now extended all the way to the Great Sea, through a network of area representatives along the Great River. Eridu City and its 300-foot-high temple to the water god slowly became background noise to their family.

Eber smiled as he remembered those years – especially the birth of his two sons, Peleg and Joktan. They were still rambunctious young boys when Azurad received an invitation to the opening ceremony for a new temple complex in Ur for the moon god, Nanna.

Called "House of Great Light," the temple was being led by a regional princess who had been promoted to a powerful new top position of *En-Priestess* – the "Lord Priestess."

All of it seemed excruciatingly ostentatious to Eber, but he went to the dedication service to support his wife – who was even less comfortable with the Nanna elements than Eber but felt she should be there for her family.

When they got to the temple, both were taken aback by the quality of the architecture and attention to details in the interior. It was five times bigger than any other temple in the area, serving as a community center as well as religious hub. The main hall was lined by statues of increasing height from back to front, with the largest in the front middle facing into the hall – Nanna himself.

In the "Great Settlement" of the moon god faith, leaders had agreed to allow a few temples in the north to continue using the name "Su-en" instead of the more common "Nanna." That allowed it to expand quickly – accelerated further by the adoption of the lunar calendar by civic and business organizations.

And it left Nanna venerated even higher than the sun god, Utu, patron god of Sippar City north of Babylon.

***

"Welcome to the House of Great Light, friends," a voice said from Eber's right. He turned to see a stunning woman, in a sheer dress with a shawl more richly embroidered in more colors than anything he had ever seen. She was at the same time sensual and commanding.

"You must be Eber, son of Shelah," she said. "I'm the Lord Priestess of Nanna and thank you so much for attending. I've heard wonderful things about your family and have been looking forward to meeting you."

Eber was transfixed by the way she seemed to flow into his path until they were six inches apart, facing. Azurad later complained she had become invisible when the High Priestess locked eyes with Eber, bowed low, kissed his hand, and said: "I am the servant of Nanna and the people of Ur."

Then she stood, still holding Eber's hand, and said, "We are here to serve any need you have, Eber. Any."

"I have a few," Azurad said, leaning in between her husband and the Lord Priestess, who smiled and took a step back. "Actually, my father – your *king* – might have some questions."

The face of the Lord Priestess turned serious. She started to speak when a loud voice called people to take their seats. It was a welcome escape that may have averted a confrontation. The Lord Priestess excused herself and walked into the main Temple amphitheater flanked by soldiers in full combat gear.

Hundreds of people were crammed into the auditorium for the service. Eber quietly tolerated the incense, incantations, and prayers to false gods. But he leaned forward with interest when an old man slowly walked to the front of the stage and picked up an antique lyre.

What happened next deeply moved Eber. The man's melodies were haunting, and his musical skill was amazing. The lyre player was soon joined by other instrumentalists – a lute, pipes, timbrels, and flutes, among others. Each song was better than the one before. Eber had never heard such skilled musicians, and he found himself thoroughly enjoying the performance.

The back of the stage with lined with opaque clay vases in a broad semicircle. Inside every jar was an oil lamp emitting smoke, each a different color. Torches were place between the jars, and the lamp smoke diffused through the torch light into a multi-colored haze that created a warm vibe. Peleg and Joktan loved the effects, and it was the first time Eber had seen them used.

At one point, Eber's mother stepped to the front in a glorious purple dress and sang a stirring rendition of a well-known folk song, "We Will Arise," with the full ensemble playing behind her. By the end, everyone in the audience was singing along, including Eber and his family.

For their finale, the lyre player began a popular Nanna hymn called "The New Moon Rises." One-by-one the other instrumentalists joined in, and by the end the entire crowd was on its feet singing. The lyrics were hopeful and never mentioned a deity, so Eber ended up humming along.

The music was followed by a short speech on how our differences should be a community's strength, not its weakness. The teacher said that true compassion was having a tolerant view of other faiths. Eber found it all thought-provoking, emotional, and inspiring.

As they were walking slowly out of the service, Eber barely noticed the milling crowd because he was deep in thought.

Maybe the Nanna movement really *was* just about helping other people, he wondered. They seemed sincere. The speaker said all people need a place where they feel safe and comfortable worshiping, no matter what their faith. He said even followers of the Creator were welcome.

After walking several minutes in silence, Azurad stopped and asked if Eber was OK. He told her how much the service had moved him and that he was re-thinking his position on Eridu City.

As Eber talked about the impact of the music, his eyes welled with tears. During the music, he had distinctly felt *ni* – what mystics describe as a "physical tingling of the flesh" when in the presence of a deity.

"Isn't *ni* the sign you are in the presence of God?" Eber asked.

Azurad took her husband's hand and smiled gently.

"No, my love," she said. "*Ni* is simply connecting with the emotions of someone else. It happens most often through artistic forms such as music, art, or poetry. Anything that helps us share the emotions of another person can bring that physical sensation of flesh-bumps."

"Then how is the presence of God different?" Eber asked.

"Oh, Eber, the presence of God is about experiencing *his* emotions, not ours," Azurad said.

"Our emotions can be manipulated. Musicians know that. *Temples* know that. They are experts at evoking emotions similar to *ni* and telling people it is God. But his presence is always with us, and *his* emotions can never be manipulated."

Before Eber could reply, the loud cry of a person in pain jolted their attention. At the end of the block, two security guards were on either side of a young woman, and they were dragging her up the street against her will. Eber remembered thinking the men looked more like street thugs than soldiers.

As the woman resisted, she broke one arm free, but a soldier took his club and hit her on the side of her head so hard she crashed to the ground, bleeding. He hit her several more times on the back of her legs while she laid helpless.

When he stopped, the woman pulled herself to all-fours, and looked up. Eber could see she was extremely thin, filthy, and wearing thread-bare clothes.

"I just wanted food for my children," she said with tears streaming down her face.

"Nobody cares," a soldier said.

The men yanked the woman to her feet, kicked her to the ground, picked her up, and kicked her to the ground again. This time, she got up and sprinted around a corner while the two soldiers stood laughing, not bothering to pursue.

***

Eber and Azurad were horrified, but everything happened so quickly they had no time to respond. They turned to ask for help, but the large crowd streaming out of the temple service seemed oblivious, as if the woman had never existed. Despite their pleas, people simply pushed past them, some muttering excuses for why they were not able to help.

Apparently, everything was more urgent than the injustice they just witnessed. Azurad turned to Eber, tightened her belt, and put her hands on her hips. Eber nodded, made sure he had clear access to his sword, and started walking, this time with his wife and sons in pursuit. As they rounded the corner of a street several blocks from the temple, they lost sight of the woman in a milling street crowd.

Down the block they could see a long line waiting to get into a building, so they approached to investigate. Glancing through the window, they saw cooks behind a table serving food to a rag-tag group of people obviously poor and homeless, representing many ages and ethnicities.

None of them wanted to go inside, so they found a window with a better view.

Azurad gasped, pointed, and said, "Eber!"

The woman who had been beaten in the street was standing in a line, with three small children in tow. The Companion was standing next to them. He slowly turned and looked directly at Azurad and Eber, but his face appeared sad.

Eber and Azurad pulled back from the window simultaneously. Both stared at the ground for several minutes in silence as they processed the day's events.

"Why would he be *here* and not *there*?" Eber whispered.

Azurad looked pensive for a moment. Then she smiled, laughed softly, and said, "Of course." Then she took his hand and led him home without saying another word.

***

Eber marveled at how much his wife had said that night. *Of course* God would be among suffering people who needed him the most. Eber's dream was beginning to make sense.

Neither was impressed with temple events after that, and neither settled for human experience over divine presence again.

Unfortunately, pulling back from temple activities quickly became a source of friction, especially since it was the centerpiece of Nimrod's new city and all major events were held there. In the end, Eridu City and its temple polarized the entire family.

The Tower in Babylon would do far worse damage.

Some in the family saw Nimrod's development projects as monuments to human determination. Others saw them as symbols of human hubris. Eber and Azurad saw them as affronts to God, because both had seen the damage done by false hope.

They tolerated nature worship, but when followers of Marduk became so zealous they took their "Generation of Sacrifice" campaign literally, Eber and Azurad had to draw the line.

Friends in Babylon told stories of sordid rituals – including one where couples would go into the wilderness, make their children watch them have sexual relations under a "sacred" oak tree, then take an infant into a ravine, where they would slash the child's throats as an offering to Marduk.

Eventually that was too much even for Nimrod, who banned the act. That led The Marduk Group to file a grievance and get a hearing with the king. They compromised by banning full child sacrifices but approving a way of "testing" the faith of young men and women. It was called "Passing Through The Fire."

Priests of Marduk would build a long, raised brick walkway, with two huge fires on either side. Children of Marduk followers had to run down the path between the super-heated fires to prove their worth. Many died trying. Though it was voluntary, parents put serious pressure on the boys to compete because those who survived were honored as heroes of the city.

The practice hit close to home when Azurad's brother ran in the Fire Challenge and survived, albeit with severe burns on his left arm that left permanent scars.

Eliezer was Nimrod's third son, and the one most like his father. Though he was the youngest of the family, Eliezer was hardly a "little" brother at 6-foot-2 and 200 pounds. Despite that, Azurad insisted on calling him "Baby Boy." She figured big sisters could do that. It was especially amusing when she had to stand on a chair to look him in the eye and say it.

For his entire life Eliezer had idolized his father and tried to emulate him – from how he hunted and dressed to how he drank and profaned God. By the time he was a teen-ager, Eliezer had become brash, overconfident, and a free-flowing fountain of sardonic humor. Just like his father. The Fire Challenge was just one example of his reckless behavior.

His course correction began on the day of the Eridu City kick-off. Though Eliezer was only 18 years old, Nimrod had promised his son a prominent role in the new project. "I made my move at your age, and it's time for you," the king said.

Eliezer sat in the second row with his family, expecting the biggest moment of his life and a spot on the stage. Nimrod followed his formal announcement of the city with appointments of officials to leadership roles in the new enterprise. One-by-one, he brought people up for awards and applause. But when Nimrod handed the podium over to a Nanna priest to close the event without calling Eliezer's name, his son became openly hostile.

In the middle of the priest's incantation, Eliezer got up from his chair, walked to the back of the room, and sulked there until the ceremony concluded. As his father slowly worked his way toward the rear exit, Eliezer became increasingly agitated. When Nimrod walked toward a nearby door to leave, Eliezer stepped in front of his father and complained loudly about being overlooked.

People nearby had no idea how to respond to Nimrod and his son shouting at each other, so they collectively pulled back. Eber and Azurad were on the other side of the room and only heard pieces of what was said, but Eliezer clearly was pushing his luck. It got so heated Nimrod finally pinned his son to a wall, drew a sword, and pressed it to his throat.

"Arrest this man for treason," Nimrod yelled. Five soldiers responded immediately. They chained Eliezer's hands and feet, then led him out.

"No way," Azurad said. She broke away from Eber and began jogging toward the exit while pulling her dagger out. Eber took a deep breath, put his hand on the hilt of his sword, and followed.

When Azurad entered the hallway leading to the courtyard, a man blocked her path, causing her to stop abruptly. It was the Companion, and he looked determined to stand his ground.

"Not yet, my child," he said. "I have much work to do *in* him before I can do much work *through* him."

Azurad was starting to speak when Eber caught up, wrapped his arms around her, and held her close. They watched helplessly as the Companion followed Eliezer and the soldiers out the door.

5

Lofty Visions

When Eber saw the sterile mud plains east of Ur for himself after years away, his emotions ranged from sadness to anger to resignation. It occurred to him that the great-great-grandson by his side would never see the Great Marsh, now a barren landscape.

Anything south of Ur between the rivers was an uninhabitable quagmire these days, and it all was avoidable.

The City of Ur was one of the first built by humans after leaving the Garden of Eden. Shem's family rebuilt the city over its foundations after The Deluge. Back then, it was near the confluence of the Great River and Gulf of Dilmun – named for the original settlement of Dilmun, halfway down the Gulf's west coast toward the Green Sea.

Ur became a key fishing and port city early, and it also was home to many in Eber's family. Even after Nimrod built up the City of Babylon, most of his relatives stayed in the south.

After the Day of Destruction in Babylon, Arpa and Rasu had joined others in Ur helping to house and feed the mass of refugees fleeing south. Eber heard many stories of local heroes who tended injured, hungry, and exhausted families. That collective compassion made Ur feel comfortable despite all the changes.

The flood of new residents had finally slowed to a trickle when Nimrod began recruiting people to his new cities in the north, especially Nineveh. As a result, Ur did not overbuild and remained warm, gentle, unhurried, and uncomplicated.

The "crazy northerners" usually just passed through, preferring the more exotic southern locales of Eridu or, for the lucky few, Dilmun with its pristine beaches and therapeutic artesian springs.

Initially Ur was settled on the west side of the Great River, where its banks quickly rose above flood levels before gradually becoming high desert.

The east side of the river back then was low-lying farmland that flooded seasonally and produced sensationally. The central portion of the "Land Between (the Rivers)" had quickly become the breadbasket of Nimrod's cities. Closer to the sea, the area was a vast and fertile marsh when Eber was growing up,

Back then, sea levels were still lowering, so the two rivers had not yet merged. Since the plains were virtually flat as they neared the Gulf of Dilmun, the area between the rivers was replete with river braiding and wetlands.

They called the combined stream through the maze of nature "The Salt River." Reeds and cattail rushes dominated the central marsh year-round. That meant its flooded grasslands and savannas were teaming with waterfowl, wildlife, and fish. And its shores were rich with poplar and willow trees.

Now it was just a big bog.

The problems started when Nimrod had proposed a "redevelopment" plan for the cities of the region. No doubt there was a need. Most settlements been built on ancient ruins, and maintenance was becoming necessary because original mud bricks were breaking down. However, ripping and replacing entire cities meant large-scale construction projects requiring extra workers – lots of them.

The burgeoning population quickly exhausted local supplies of key building materials. Quality timber became especially hard to find, so people resorted to using lower-quality wood for basic furniture and fuel – including tamarisk and acacia.

To feed the growing crowds, residents dug canals and irrigation systems with little planning. In the process, they drained much of the marsh water and dumped human excrement into the rivers. That left dead vegetation and sick marsh-dwellers for miles downstream.

Then workers dug out tons of mud and reeds to make new bricks for buildings, which caused rampant erosion and weathering. At the same time, many of the birds, reptiles, and other wildlife in the Great Marsh starved or were hunted to extinction. After the Tower fell and its debris washed downstream, the area became a dump site.

***

Eber pondered the irony of urban renewal resulting in rural ruin. It also had caused spiritual ruin.

That downward spiral started when Nimrod formally announced the Tower with a gala event in Babylon. Its kickoff tagline set the tone: "Heaven For Everyone."

Arpa scornfully called it "Heaven For Sale." Its mission statement was a declaration that people could attain greatness on their own, and they did not need God's help. The Tower would prove that all human beings deserved direct access to paradise.

People embraced it en masse. When Nimrod said they could be happy through their own courage, many saw the Tower as the ultimate self-validation. Unfortunately, Nimrod did not really want to *reach* God; he just wanted to be more *famous* than God.

The strategy was sheer genius. In the end, Nimrod rarely had to conquer anyone. People usually just promoted him from city manager to king, trading their dependence on gods to dependence on Nimrod.

It was a lawless time, so Nimrod's "Safe Cities" pledge seemed worth giving up a few freedoms to help achieve. However, few people anticipated his immediate and dramatic increase in military presence, which included his elite Palace Guard. Nimrod said it was just a short-term action to deliver on his law-and-order platform, but he quickly changed the government from a network of city-states to an absolute dictatorship ruled by fear, despotism, and force of arms.

It did not start out that way. In the early years, much of the Tower construction labor was done by farmers during flood season. Nimrod sold it as an opportunity to make money when they could not work their fields. At the same time, many learned second skill sets, such as metal working and masonry.

As people prospered, managers began looking for new ways to boost productivity, and profitability. A key development was invention of a process for baking mud bricks in a furnace until they were hard as stone, and then sealing them with waterproof bitumen mortar – the same black, gooey substance used by Noah.

"Burnt bricks" became so in-demand, several large companies formed to mass-produce them.

Unfortunately, after the Tower fell, tons of the brick residue flushed down the Great River and ended up in a massive toxic slurry where the Great Marsh had been.

Eber sighed and considered the contrast. When his family had first arrived in the area so many years ago, they often went hunting and fishing on that side of the river. Now it was desolate and infested with insects.

"Can we go now?" a young voice asked. Eber chuckled. His great-great grandson had respectfully waited at least 20 minutes before breaking the silence, which was commendable since Eber probably had asked Arpa the same question a hundred times. After all, he had served in a similar role as his grandfather's hiking partner and helper for years.

Now one of Peleg great-grandsons was walking with him.

***

Eber sighed at the thought of his oldest son. Peleg had received his father's work ethic and his mother's intellect. He had special gifts in administration and comprehending other languages, which made him invaluable in the Second Sending. But Peleg was only 13 when his Grandfather Shelah broke the news about the Tower.

Eber's family had been invited to an art exhibit in a side room at "House of the Great Light," the main Nanna temple complex in Ur. Shelah was displaying bronze relief work, which was to be auctioned off as part of a fundraising effort for a new arts center in the Central City. It all seemed like a safe diversion from Nimrod controversies, so Eber and Azurad agreed to attend. After about an hour of browsing through the exhibits, they decided the beautiful pottery work alone had been worth the trip.

Then they found Shelah's display, and both stopped walking at the same time.

In front of them was a large gold-plated statue of the moon god Nanna, depicted this time as a male bovine with a man's head, long beard, and royal headdress. It was laying down in a resting position.

What is this fixation with golden calves? Eber remembered asking himself sarcastically.

The internal humor was little consolation. As Eber scanned his father's pieces lining the wall, his heart sank. Each was a representation of a different god. On the front wall was a large sign that said: "A Community of Faiths."

Azurad spoke first. "Where are the boys?"

Eber glanced around and did not see his sons, so they went separate ways down the hall searching. He saw a light in a side room and went to investigate. A servant standing at the door nodded as he approached and extended his hand to enter.

"Eber, what a pleasant surprise," the Lord Priestess said as he walked in.

Eber stopped, startled. This was her office, home, and place of ... well, *consorting*.

She was sitting on a beautiful couch facing a low table that had several chairs on the other side. In one corner of the room was a small cedar desk, with intricate carvings of various deities and a matching stool. In another corner was an elevated platform with a large bed, surrounded by insect netting and covered by some of the most exquisite tapestry Eber had ever seen.

"Come, sit, and talk for a moment," she said, patting the open spot next to her on the couch.

Eber was so surprised he had no answer other than mumbling something about looking for his boys. She glanced at her servant, nodded slightly, and he left the room – closing the door discreetly behind him. Eber was confused and not sure what to say, so he stood stationary and said nothing. After a few moments of awkward silence, the Lord Priestess smiled, stood up, and walked toward Eber.

She stopped just short of him, lit a candle, and placed it on a wall shrine directly behind him – purposely brushing his arm with her breast, slowly.

Eber was instantly and painfully uncomfortable in body, mind, and spirit. He began to respond, but the woman had turned and was walking back to her couch. She sat down and spoke before Eber had a chance to say he needed to leave.

"People often have a narrow view about what we do here, but they often change their minds when they experience it for themselves," she said. "The gods created sexual intimacy so we can feel and share the unveiled emotions of another person. We believe making love is for mutual pleasure, not just for procreation. When it is with someone you enjoy and admire, it can be heaven on earth."

The Lord Priestess leaned forward. "I like and respect you, Eber. Have you ever encountered a woman who practices sexual pleasure as a divine mission?"

Eber knew there was no safe answer to that question. Sex had become a component of religious rituals early in the growth of polytheism, so he had heard more than a few wild stories growing up as Shelah's son.

Some sects required female adherents to serve stints as a temple prostitute, providing favors in exchange for "donations" to their temple – not for the sex, of course.

Other groups required married women once in their lifetime to have intercourse with a stranger for a temple donation, and some of the less attractive women were stuck there for years waiting to get selected from the crowd.

That attitude was a sign of the times. Street prostitution had exploded along with the population growth, so it quickly became seen as an expected feature of urban life. It became so widespread the cities began to standardize how to identify a prostitute.

The most common signal was a woman standing topless, cupping her breasts. In Babylon, prostitutes also often wore belts and necklaces made of beads, silver, or gold. The more jewelry, the higher the class of prostitute.

Eber noticed the Lord Priestess was subtly wearing numerous braided gold and silver belts embedded with hard-to-get precious stones over her dress.

"I take your silence as a no answer, Eber" the Lord Priestess said. "Are you familiar with Sacred Marriage?"

If Eber had been uncomfortable with the conversation before then, the topic of Sacred Marriage made him perspire.

***

Everyone in the temple network knew about the rite. In their multi-god mythology, the fertility goddess Ishtar had sexual relations with the shepherd god, Dumzi. Through that act, a "divine fertility energy" was released on the land, ensuring good crops and productive livestock that year.

The Sacred Marriage liturgy culminated with two people simulating that coupling. Each time one of the major cities swore in a new king or high priest, they would hold a Sacred Marriage to invoke a blessing for a fruitful land.

The High Priestess would play the role of "Ishtar" in the re-creation, and the king or priest would play the role of "Dumuzi." After a mock wedding, they would retire for a night of sex. It struck Eber the High Priestess probably had slept with countless partners in the name of piety.

"As son of Shelah, I am quite familiar with Sacred Marriage," Eber said, continuing to stand as she sat. "To me it always seemed like a lot of effort for one night of sex."

The Lord Priestess leaned back, laughed genuinely, and said, "Some put in more effort than others, certainly."

This time it was Eber's turn to laugh, but he also had to find a way out of that room, and quickly.

"Actually, Lord Priestess, I already *am* in a sacred marriage – with Azurad, daughter of King Nimrod," Eber said. "And the princess expects me *every* night."

The Lord Priestess stood, dropped her embroidered shawl on the couch, and took a step forward. She was wearing a sheer, tightly fitting ankle-length silk dress that clung sensuously to her figure. This woman was gorgeous and dressed to attract attention.

It worked, so Eber took a deep breath, then took a step back.

"Kings and high priests have been with me for one night, and each said it was the best night of their lives," she said. "If nobody gets hurt in the process of two consenting adults pleasing each other, why deny yourself the joy?"

Eber knew it was time to draw boundaries – or at least deflect the conversation – right *now*.

"Lord Priestess, every night with Azurad has been the best night of my life, "Eber said. "And you are wrong about one thing. Somebody *would* get hurt – my wife – and I would not do that to her. Now if you will please excuse me, I need to find my family."

Eber turned to see Azurad standing silently in an open doorway, with her hands on her hips – her right hand resting on her dagger scabbard, never a good sign. He had no idea how long she had been there, but Eber walked to his wife, paused, took her dagger hand in his, and led her out the door.

Halfway down the hall, Azurad stopped, stepped to face Eber, leaned into him, and gave him a long, slow kiss.

"Well done, my love," she said. "Now let's go home."

That sounded perfect to Eber, so he quickly located their two sons watching a man juggling three wicker balls nearby, while Azurad went to say good-bye to their family.

They met back in the hallway and were almost out the door when a voice behind them said, "Eber!"

Shelah was walking toward them, quickly and with a smile.

"I'm so glad you could come," he said as he opened his arms to hug Azurad. Then he looked down at his grandsons and said loudly, "Boys!"

Peleg and Joktan warmly embraced their grandfather, with much laugher. Finally, Shelah turned and greeted Eber. Then he asked the question his son had been dreading:

"I'm still perfecting my bull figures, but what do you think of my newest work?"

Eber said something about the intricate bronze engraving work. Azurad mentioned how favorably it compared to those in the temple main lobby. Joktan wanted to know if he could ride on the Nanna statue. But 13-year-old Peleg cut to the chase:

"Why did you make a fake god?" he asked.

***

Eber was mortified and proud at the same time, but before he could respond Shelah leaned down and began lecturing the boy on how important it was to be respectful of all the faiths in the area. Peleg cut him off in mid-sentence.

"Grandfather, I know there are lots of gods, but isn't there just one *real* one?"

Shelah looked irritated, crossed his arms, and said, "Well Peleg, we don't judge people for having different beliefs here."

Azurad stepped forward, draped an arm over her son's shoulder, and said, "And that's enough of such weighty subjects when we have so much artistic beauty around us tonight, my father-in-law."

Shelah saw the resolute look on Azurad's face, got the point, directed the two boys to a table with snacks, turned back to Azurad, and changed the subject. Not in a good way.

"This actually may be my last Ur exhibit for some time," Shelah said. He glanced around, then motioned for them to join him in a quiet corner.

"Nimrod has a new project that will be his biggest yet, and he wants me to do the medallion designs. He sees it as his apex legacy – a tower to heaven rising through the clouds above the plains of Babylon."

Eber immediately was lost in a churn of thoughts, but they kept coming back to a mental image of the tower in his dream. Before he could speak, his father continued.

"You know, Nimrod talks about Eber when he's pitching the Tower to investors. He says he got the idea years ago but did not think much about it until you had that dream. He felt your vision was confirmation he was supposed to build it."

Eber started to challenge the assumption he had anything to do with Nimrod's aspirations, but he hesitated. Getting into a debate here over a building not yet even designed seemed like a no-win proposition. Besides, anchor projects like temple ziggurats were just a symbol of a broader concern Eber had – the cities themselves.

God had been explicit to Noah and his family about dispersing throughout in the earth, and not congregating in a few locations. Arpa believed God did it for our good. "Cities are just smelly disease traps waiting to become disasters," he said.

Certainly, the track record of cities had been abysmal to that point in human history. Eber was about to weigh in when his father started talking again.

"I'm actually very excited about the Tower idea," Shelah said. "I know you may think it is just ego, but there are some solid reasons for building it."

Then Shelah launched into a discourse on the value of Babylon as regional economic center and the Tower project as a hedge against future global floods. It quickly began to feel like a well-rehearsed sales script when he talked about *The Foundation of Heaven on Earth* being a magnificent symbol of a new era.

"The Tower will usher in a glorious time of innovation and renewed faith in the human spirit," Shelah said. "And it will be King Nimrod's crowning achievement."

Eber knew better. He had been in enough conversations with Nimrod to know his father-in-law was driven by painful insecurity. He needed to have more and do more, all the time. Each city or monument had to be bigger than the one before. It would never stop. The Tower was just a high-profile way to raise money and support for even more projects.

***

The pattern had been established when the Nimrod built up his four central cities – Erech, Akkad, Calneh, and his capitol, Babylon. He would increase taxes, import bondservants and materials into the area, disrupt the local economies, and make the residents rely on him for most of their basic needs.

With concentrated power, he got things done quickly by force. But the consequences included cruel labor conditions, worker unrest, harsh government responses, and unjust imprisonments – or even execution for many. That was amplified exponentially during the Tower construction. Because of its height, near the end it took weeks to carry construction materials to the top, forcing workers to leave home for years at a time.

Finishing the Tower became everything to everyone involved. Pregnant women were forced to have babies on the job, wrap them in their aprons, and then continue working the rest of their shifts. If a worker dropped a single brick, all would pause to weep over it. But if someone died, no one was allowed to even look at the dead body.

Despite the institutional cruelty, Nimrod had an uncanny ability to charm people into believing there was a higher and noble purpose in each project – something so grand you *had* to be involved. The Tower gave him a lofty vision of historic proportions. He knew people would love it, and they did.

The original goal of the Tower was to reach heaven and the Creator, but a "Vision Committee" formed by Nimrod expanded the mission to include all faiths and the seven heavens they represented. Its objective quickly morphed from reaching heaven to conquering it and overthrowing God.

Soon after Nimrod declared war on heaven, people and whole families split into three factions. The first said they would ascend into heaven and exile God. The second said they would ascend to heaven and place their own gods there to serve. The third said they would ascend to heaven and kill God with bows and spears.

The aggressive approach picked up steam about halfway through the construction, when a dozen security workers got drunk one night after work, decided to kill God on their own, went out onto the Level Four terrace, and shot arrows into the sky. Some of the arrows came down with blood on their shafts, which resulted in a popular tavern song called, "We Have Slain the Ones in Heaven."

***

Nimrod eventually ordered the sign at the main entrance changed from "Gate of God" to "Gate of the Gods" – ostensibly to be inclusive of all gods, but really to exclude the Creator from his plans. Nobody cared because everything he touched seemed to prosper.

Nimrod's compelling vision of connected cities on the plain of Shinar had driven rapid progress. It fueled development of new economies, technologies, and agricultural systems to support clustered populations. Other new disciplines included writing, astronomy, computational systems, and construction design techniques that included the invention of geometric calculations.

The era also produced some intriguing new musical instruments that had caught Eber's attention.

However, advancements in so many areas so quickly came with a high price. Small farms could not compete with undercutting of labor costs, sophisticated new irrigation systems, far-reaching trade agreements, and modern land management techniques. Local businesses ended up at the bottom of the ensuing social stratification.

The biggest problem emerged during the expansion in the north. Many imported workers had developed their own languages and religions by then. Those traditions had to be respected, which meant communication broke down and beliefs became fragmented early. Arpa often joked that the Great Confusion began years before the Tower fell.

Nobody was confused the night Shelah told them about plans to build the Tower. Nimrod would not stop until it was finished, no matter what the cost.

***

Eber's thoughts were interrupted by Azurad's voice thanking Shelah for inviting the family to his exhibit. He forced himself to re-engage, cordially thank his father for inviting them, and tell everyone how much he had enjoyed it. But Eber's mind was far away, and Azurad knew it.

When they got home and the boys were in bed, they moved into the kitchen and out of earshot. Eber sat at the table while Azurad poured two glasses of wine, handed Eber one, then sat down across from him.

"We have a tough decision coming up," she said. "You know my father will pressure you to be involved in the Tower."

"I know," Eber said. "But that means he will pressure *you* to be involved, too. This choice will shape our relationship with your family for years to come, so what do you want to do, my love?"

Azurad took a sip of wine, got up, walked over to an open window, and stood staring out with her hands on the sill.

"You always put me and our family ahead of your own needs, Eber, so I trust you," she said. "What does my husband think we should do?"

Eber got up, walked over to his wife, stood behind her, wrapped his arms around her waist, and pulled her close.

"We should obey the Lord," he whispered.

Azurad smiled grimly and nodded. Both knew they would need to travel far away to escape involvement in the Tower. The family had a long journey ahead.

Through the window, they could see the Companion waiting at their front gate, leaning on his walking staff.

6

Stairway To Heaven

Decades after the Tower fell, people were still talking about the awe of seeing it for the first time. *The Foundation of Heaven On Earth* made a lifelong visual impression. Even while under construction, it was a monster.

When Eber made his first trip back to Ur and passed through Babylon, he expected a large work site. He did not expect to see the Tower from a ridge 10 miles away.

Eber had taken his family north to evade Nimrod's wrath over his refusal to help with the Tower, so contact with family in the south was rare at first. Ending up in Harran City, two months away by foot, did not help.

However, when Nimrod moved further northeast along the Arrow River to Nineveh, Eber finally felt it was safe to visit Arpa in Ur. He also was able to reconnect with trading partners along the Great River and negotiate new deals.

Over the ensuing years, Eber made several trips to the southern cities. Each time he passed through Babylon, the Tower grew bigger, and faster than he expected. When completed, it became the top wonder of the known world, literally.

Azurad and Eber had received regular updates on the progress of the Tower and knew it would be large, but it ended up beyond comparison. On their first trip to Babylon five years into construction, it already dominated the landscape behind the Temple of Bel at more than 500 feet tall – and they had just finished the foundation of Level One.

Eber remembered being taken aback by the sheer footprint of its base, almost half the size of the city itself. Nearby was a separate mountain of mud bricks. Those were being taken into buildings with furnaces on each end, where workers baked the bricks, coated them with bitumen, glazed many with various colors, and stacked them outside for workers to haul away.

"That *is* a big building," Azurad said. "But then it has been five years since we saw it last."

Both flashed weak smiles. The past years had been tough for their family, but at least this was a major distraction, so they just stood staring at it for a long time from a plateau to the northwest.

The Tower made its biggest impact after completion, when they saw it up-close during the family's seven-day, six-night tour spent ascending and walking through the entire 10-level structure – with Azurad's brother Hunor as a guide.

It may not have been a tower to heaven, but it was a Tower big enough to get their attention. And God's.

***

As daughter of the king, Azurad received a courtesy invitation to tour the Tower five years before its dedication. The building was complete already, but it took years to clean out construction equipment, dismantle worker housing, herd animals down, and move in all the new furniture and creative accoutrements that made its design much more than decoration.

Azurad, Eber, and their sons arrived at the Tower in a horse-drawn carriage – meaning it came from a royal stable. They had stayed at a small inn on the West Side to avoid any family issues. In the morning, they walked to the Great River and took a rope-drawn ferry across to the East Side. The carriage and driver were waiting to take them into the city.

As they approached the city's East Wall main gate, its sign set the tone: "Babylon, Gate of the Gods."

Eber simply shook his head, because he knew hyperbole permeated every part of Babylonian culture. For decades, the dominant building in Babylon had been the "The Temple Whose Top Is Lofty," dedicated to Marduk, patron god of the city.

The Marduk Group retained rights to the temple on the top of the new building, but they lost the overall Tower design bid to Nanna International. Nimrod's connections to the High Priestess had remained strong, and moon god followers offered to build a structure so tall it would dwarf "Top Is Lofty." Besides, new money trumped old money when it came to dreaming big.

The Tower of Babylon officially was named "The Temple of the Foundation of Heaven and Earth," a title obviously stitched together by a large committee.

Most people simply called it "The Tower."

Its top level would feature the new temple of Marduk, where he apparently could watch over his city more efficiently from a higher perch. To appease traditionalists, the temple would play homage to the old building's name with the new title, "Temple Whose Top Is *Most* Lofty." The compromise was well received.

As important as the city was to Nimrod, the Tower became his legacy, like it or not. While it stood, it was magnificent. Eber was impressed before he and the family even got off their wagon to start the tour.

A cuneiform guide listed key features and attractions on Level One, as well as its impressive specs, but even those record-crushing numbers did little justice to its scope.

To start, the main wall was 75 feet thick, 400 feet tall, and took a week to walk around. It was constructed with burnt bricks that were formed into large rectangular blocks and filled with earth. Bitumen was used to coat the bricks and served as a waterproof mortar.

Grandmother Rasu made planters in her garden like that, Eber thought randomly at the time.

Each side of the Tower's wall had 25 gates embedded in its 20-mile length, with huge doors of cast bronze that were decorated with elaborate engravings.

The cart stopped for inspection at one of the 100 gates, and Eber made the mistake of looking up – at the Tower rising thousands of feet above him. He started to feel nauseous, heard his wife chuckling, and turned to see her grinning.

"Looking forward to getting up there? Azurad asked playfully.

"Let's just get there," he said gruffly. The rest of the family laughed as the wagon pulled through the "Gate of the Gods" and into a world of wonder.

Level One: Seven Heavens Plaza

When Eber's family entered the Level One main courtyard, they finally got to see the magnificent spiral road winding up and around the outside of the Tower to its top.

"The Great Nimrod Way" – called "The NimWay" by most – was the key route up the Tower. It was wide enough to handle wagons, animals, and people. But it ended up being used for much more.

When construction reached the upper levels, it took workers almost a day just to get to the site, under the best of circumstances. Also, near the top crews were having difficulty breathing in the high altitude. Eber had to credit engineers for a clever design solution:

They used The NimWay for multiple purposes.

In most places, the road was wide enough to build huts and even cabins along its perimeter. Those were used to house workers and animals. Each had an earthen roof for growing herbs, vegetables, and feed. People now could live close to their job sites, making construction much more efficient – though it still took about a century to finish.

On lower levels, the NimWay was wide enough to add full gardens. Some spots even had short-form fields, which were used to grow grain for humans and animals.

A group of managers who called themselves the "Tower Dream Team" had workers build rest areas near the entrance to each level off the NimWay – with a mini-terrace, benches, water station, food shop, and relief areas for those making the ascent. The "Oasis" patios became wildly popular among tourists and residents alike.

Before the Tower fell, one of the highlights in Babylon was "The NimWay Run," which drew top athletes from far away to participate in a race to the top and back to the bottom. Watching from an Oasis patio was considered the best seat in the Tower.

Eber laughed. He remembered watching the NimWay Run one year and being amazed by the endurance of the participants. The day of their tour, he got winded just getting off the cart and walking across the broad Level One courtyard.

His family continued through an arched walkway and into a large open plaza, with walls and columns rising three stories on all sides to a roof that obviously doubled as the floor of the next level. A raised stage was at one end of the room, with a small group of musicians playing familiar local folk songs.

The "Seven Heavens Plaza" was named for an old-school sect that had purchased the naming rights. They believed the sky was a series of seven domes, and that the Tower would pierce through the top one and reach God. Most people thought The Sons of Seven were bizarre, but they had some wealthy members in a city that was more than happy to take their money.

Most residents called Level One "People's Plaza," because so many families came for its field games during festival season. The Plaza was especially popular with visitors to the city who wanted to experience the Tower but not make the grueling trip to the top.

Shops, cafes, smoking rooms, and taverns lined the walls of the plaza. Companions were available in the tunnels under the plaza, women or men. And they were not hard to spot.

Azurad ushered the family toward "Seven Heavens Temple," a multi-faith building accessible to the public. Inside the temple was a central nave, with aisles running along both sides. Closet-sized areas for priests lined the walls, which were decorated with detailed reliefs depicting various scenes of gods in action.

At the far end of the room was a raised platform, with a mud-brick table for sacrificing animals and vegetables. A curtain blocked a door to an inner court in the back that was off limits to the public.

Seven "Divine" rooms branched off from the main sanctuary area. The first was for Marduk to share with his wife. There also were rooms for the scribe god and his wife, the water god, the light god, the god of heaven, and of course one for top god Enlil.

The seventh room was especially sacred. The "House of the Bed," contained a large bed that was used for Sacred Marriages.

"I think we just found the Lord Priestess' new office," Azurad quipped when she saw it.

Since People's Plaza was much more vibrant and upbeat, they headed back outside. Their sons loved the energy and would have been happy staying there all day. But by then Eber was over 200 years old, so he had an excuse for wanting a less crowded location.

Level Two: Public Business Plaza

Hunor led them to large and broad steps on the east side of the Plaza level that rose to Level Two. At the top of the steps, the outer wall of the Tower became a five-story circle. Its top was a circular platform, with a smaller square platform inset in its middle that was several miles long on each side.

That block base served as the foundation for the Tower's upper levels. It was surrounded by a park with a popular zoo that could be reached easily via a system of free wagons between the first two levels.

From Level Two, the Tower rose in ever-smaller slices to its top. However, most people never went beyond the parkway on Level Two – dryly named "Public Business Plaza" because it was designed for single-day visitors. It became much more.

The gardens, trees, and wildlife were worth a visit to the Level Two terrace, which also offered numerous spots for people to sit and enjoy unblocked views of the city and Great River valley.

Inside the buildings ringing the Level Three base, visitors encountered a loud and crowded maze of inns, cafes, taverns, markets, tourist shops, and brothels. Their sons took a special interest in the women cupping their breasts in back corridors, so Azurad pointedly told her brother it was time to go higher. From Public Business Plaza, you had three options when ascending.

First, you could take steep steps dubbed the "Stairway To Heaven" in an 87-foot-square ventilation shaft that rose straight up the very center of the structure, from floor to roof.

The Stairway was built to be maintenance steps, hugging the walls of the shaft and rising thousands of feet in an exhausting and dizzying series of switchbacks, with doors at each level. It was mostly used by service workers and couriers, though some extreme athletes used it to train for the NimWay Run,

Second, you could walk or run The NimWay all the way to the top. Few people did that just for fun.

Third, and most common, you could ride a camel, donkey, horse, or cart up The NimWay to the top – though once you reached Level Nine, you still had to walk the final steps up.

That meant going all the way to Level Ten required an ability to walk, good lungs, and comfort with heights. Eber scored fine in the first two areas, but he was not looking forward to the final part of the ascent. He did not *fear* heights. He just did not like feeling vulnerable if it could be avoided.

Of course, he was thinking ahead. First, he needed to reach Level Three. The rest of the family already had made the decision to walk this stretch, and they all needed to burn off some energy from the cart trip, so they sent the wagon ahead and started up The NimWay.

Eber was not surprised when Azurad, Peleg, and Joktan bolted ahead. He knew they would run out of steam or get distracted, and his slow-but-steady strategy would result in him passing them by the end.

Level Three: Private Business Plaza

Though all levels had similar structural layouts, each had different uses that produced widely varied interior designs. Level Three blended a little of everything and was relatively calm because it was the "Private Business Level," another towering example of mediocrity in naming.

Eber had many friends working on that level, so he spent much of the afternoon introducing his family to the wholesalers and traders who dominated the floor.

Level Three was the last area openly accessible to the public, so anyone going higher needed a valid "signature stone" – a small, intricately carved cylinder stone used as a seal or signature because it was small and could not be copied easily. If you had one, you could access the Private Business Lounge and pass through a security gate guarding The NimWay section leading to the upper levels.

"Security Stones" were not cheap, and there was a two-month wait to get one – unless you were the king's daughter, of course.

On a patio outside the office building, about 50 people were standing in line to enter a large corner tent, which served as a "Career Development Center" for the many positions available in a facility that size. Managers would conduct screenings, place people in the jobs and training, and offer translation services for those coming in from other lands via boats off the Gulf of Dilmun.

Since it was getting late in the day, the family settled into a nice but simple local inn booked by Hunor, amusingly named "The Ark" and decorated with murals of animals on boats.

Level Four: The Temple Co-Op

Azurad had been dreading the second day, because Level Four was the "Temple Co-Op," a loose coalition of diverse religions, including Nanna International. However, when she was told at breakfast that the Lord Priestess was currently up north in Resen, the "Great City" between Nineveh and Calah, Azurad relaxed significantly.

"What, we missed the Sacred Spouse?" she said dryly. "What a disappointment. I was so looking forward to visiting."

Eber had been more concerned about his wife's dagger than her words, but all fears proved to be unfounded when they got up to Level Four. Although it was filled with polytheistic trinkets, the level also included some of the most fun they had on the tour.

The Co-Op was a ring of stations hosted by various religions. Most of the booths had miniature altars and shrines, with carved images and reliefs available for sale. But many also had creative games and activities, including a zoo the entire family enjoyed.

Inside the buildings around the Level Five base, the familiar layout had a smaller footprint used by temple administrators and minor idol-makers. Each had a team in a booth along the wall, with runners carrying instructions to the Stairway.

Outside the building entrance, small groups of musicians were performing. Also, artisans had set up stations and were demonstrating how to work with metals, wood, clay, stone, and precious stones.

Today, the "Artist Way" amphitheater was featuring a new technique. It used a potter's wheel to shape clay into an idol, then baked it hard in an oven using extremely high temperatures. Many came out with unusual and creative patterns. Azurad wanted to spend more time studying the process, so Eber took his sons to find something to eat on the veranda.

By mid-day, the family was getting restless and ascended to one of the Tower's most expensive and lavish areas.

Level Five: The Dwellings, at The Tower

Early in the Tower planning, Nimrod realized it was going to cost a whole lot more than he originally thought. That budget crisis resulted in a drive to reduce expenses and increase funding.

He cut expenses by hiring low-cost workers.

He boosted revenues every way he could – starting with sponsorships, higher rents, and ingenious new forms of taxes. The most audacious money-maker was Level Five's "The Dwellings, at The Tower." Note the communications team was adamant about capitalizing "The" twice.

The Dwellings was a collaborative project concocted by a team of developers from five cities called The Sacred Valley Group. They signed a 10-year lease on the entire fifth level to build a franchise focused on housing – targeting upper-income priests and temple employees working on the level below, as well as operations managers from the level above.

Anyone working above Level Three was classified as highly compensated, so Sacred Valley created an opulent community of townhouses, corner markets, parks, gardens, pet grounds, schools, and recreational facilities.

A masterpiece of fusion architecture, The Dwellings wove together modern and natural elements. The central building resembled a large green mountain, constructed of mud bricks but overlayed with an ascending series of tiered gardens that included a wide variety of trees, vines, and shrubs.

The family wanted to spend time in hot pools overlooking the city, but Hunor was anxious to get through the next two levels, so they loaded on the cart and headed up The NimWay.

Level Six: Tower Operations Center

Level Six was boring. To Eber, "The Tower Operations Center" meant a bunch of middle-management bureaucrats. It was exactly that. But it also included maintenance and security offices as well as building operations, so it ended up being both the busiest and least interesting level.

Everyone seemed very industrious and focused on their tasks, so the family quickly and quietly walked through their offices. The only noise came from young couriers darting in and out of a small door leading to the Stairway. Eber later learned they were taking notes and edicts from upper levels to the masses below.

The saving grace of Level Six was its famous restaurant, "Middle of the Tower." Hunor had promised Eber it had the best roast pheasant in the region, and he had to agree.

After dinner, they checked in at an inn for traveling executives, which was functional like the rest of the level. The next morning, they slept in, had a late lunch, then moved on.

Level Seven: The Nimrod Institute

When the family got to Level Seven, they took a break. It gave Eber time to reflect. This was the level where his father had worked as a consultant for the Tower leadership – a group of strategic thinkers who formed "The Nimrod Institute."

Supposedly they focused on solving big problems facing Babylon and the Tower. The Institute attracted experts from business, government, the sciences, astrology, the military, and influential religions such as Nanna International.

It became a template for think tanks, future cities, and temple organizations. Unfortunately, Level Seven also was notorious for producing almost nothing of practical value, while spending very much in the process.

It never really mattered, though. Anything that linked policy with action was vetoed by the king anyway. For some reason, that had never bothered Eber's father. Shelah was too proud of being a Level Seven "expert" to worry about measurable results. The Institute also had the best employee cafeteria in the Tower.

"Thinking about your father?" Azurad asked.

"Yes, he was in his element here," Eber said. "A bunch of smart guys thinking up new ways to do nothing. But my father loved working with creative deep thinkers. He even came up with the first city medallions here."

The sun was lowering in the western sky, so the tour team guided them to a cluster of apartments built into the wall of the central building. There they spent the night at the home of Azurad's childhood best friend – though with all the excitement, none of them slept much.

The next morning, they had breakfast, loaded onto the cart, and wound their way up the increasingly smaller levels.

Level Eight: Babylon Dream

Level Eight was a much smaller multipurpose area designed to solve the problem of combining residential and business areas. Planners felt that by mixing housing with commercial activities, people would not have to travel up and down the Tower. Unfortunately, the idea was slow to catch on.

A well-known mixed-use development group named "Babylon Dream" took on the contract, to mixed results. Many of the stations were vacant, in part because of the effort it took to get up there and in part because a post-construction recession had constricted consumer spending.

The level was mainly used for its apartments, with small restaurants, retail shops, markets, and bazaars supporting the residents. People with jobs on Level Seven often rented sleeping space on Level Eight – at a steep premium – to shorten their commute walk from the ground levels.

Eber's family stayed in a rustic corner Bed & Breakfast Inn for the night, falling asleep to the sound of a light rain.

Level Nine: Royal Plaza

The Royal Plaza was the most expensive place in the world to live. It also was Azurad's favorite part of the tour because it included top-quality spas with hot mineral baths on the terrace, featuring a spectacular view of the Zagros Mountains.

The weather was beautiful, and the family needed a break, so Eber found the cottage they had rented among a grove of palm trees and checked in early.

They spent the rest of the day relaxing.

Also, Azurad let her brother know in uncertain terms that her family would not attend the portion of the tour that went through lavish apartments designed specifically for use in ritual sex. The men were disappointed, but she expected that response. They would have to settle for a boring day with the princess instead.

Level Ten: Eden Plaza (and The Needle)

The final morning, they got up early to see the exclusive top level, called "Eden Plaza." This invitation-only section was operated by The Marduk Group, so security was tight, credentials were required, and you had to be escorted by guards up the final section of The NimWay to a gold-plated gate with a large relief of the sun god.

The family stepped through the gate into the most beautiful park they had ever seen. The entire level was a terrace of paths winding through orchards, vineyards, fragrant flower gardens, and aviaries with exotic birds. Around the edges were benches under lattices for reclining and meditation, with unprecedented views any direction.

A small building dedicated to Marduk stood in the center of Eden Plaza. "The Temple Whose Top Is *Most* Lofty" was considered to be "holy of holies" by Marduk priests.

The temple had several rooms with richly covered furniture, gold-plated tables, altars, shrines, candles, oil lamps, stringed instruments on stands, incense censers, and other sacred accessories. In the largest room, a gold table was placed next to a luxurious couch. Hunor explained that the High Priestess of Marduk would spend one night a year alone in the room, as a symbolic coupling with her god.

A three-sided, gold-plated spire protruded from the middle of the temple and narrowed to a point about 50 feet above the roof. It was the top of the Tower, and though the official name was "Arrow of Marduk," most people called it "The Needle."

Royal astronomers spent many nights making observations from its platform.

The Needle had a sign identical to the city entrance: "Gate of the Gods." Azurad stood staring at the nameplate for a long time before Eber finally asked if she was OK.

"If this place is God's gate, why isn't *he* here," she said. Eber had no answer. Then he realized he had not seen the Companion since crossing the river six days earlier.

***

The family descended to the Level Nine inn for the night, too tired to talk much. Early the next morning, they ate a quick breakfast and loaded onto carts for the grueling eight-hour trip down The NimWay.

They arrived back at People's Plaza late that afternoon. A carriage took them to the river, where they caught the ferry back to the West Side. Then the family disembarked and quietly walked single file down the ramp, up a trail, and toward their inn.

Azurad abruptly stopped, turned, and asked her sons to wait for a few minutes. Eber looked puzzled, but his eyes followed her gaze. The Companion was standing at the top of the hill. She took Eber's hand and led him toward the man.

"Why weren't you at the Tower," Azurad asked boldly when they got close.

The Companion smiled, leaned on his staff, and said, "What makes you think I wasn't there?"

"We didn't see you," she said.

"Even when you don't see me or feel me, I am always with you," the Companion said. "Remember the Creator does not dwell in Towers made by human hands."

A comforting current of wind swirled around them, then subsided. It was more than *ni* because it went beyond emotion to a sense that someone else was physically *present*. Eber had missed that experience. It had seemed "strange" at first, but now the Companion's presence felt intimately familiar.

"If God doesn't live in the Tower, where is he?" a voice asked. Eber and Azurad turned around to see Peleg trailing them, with Joktan standing just behind his brother.

Peleg sees him! Eber remembered thinking.

The Companion smiled and leaned against his staff, so Peleg started to step forward, but he hesitated and edged next to his mother instead.

"You do not have to look far to find God, Peleg," the Companion said. "The Creator longs to walk with you every day, so he is always right beside you. Your family will need him for the challenges ahead."

A strong and cold gust of wind suddenly hit them so hard it blew off Eber's hat and knocked down a sign near them pointing to the Tower. Azurad quickly threw her cloak around her shivering sons, and Eber helped. When they turned back, the Companion was gone.

7

Momentary Glory

After walking eight weeks from Harran to Babylon for the much-hyped Day of Dedication, Eber was just relieved to get there. The Tower had lost its novelty long ago, having taken a century to build and another five years to prepare a kick-off event almost as imperious as the building itself.

"I can't believe they finally got it cleaned out," Azurad said as she surveyed the city and the massive structure that dominated its skyline from a plateau to the northwest.

The Tower had taken four times longer to complete than the king's "experts" had predicted. Eber figured the protracted construction timeline had been mostly due to Nimrod building up the city and the Tower at the same time. People later forgot cities were the most important part of the pagan ecosystem Nimrod created, down to mandating the symbols to be placed on the inside of every doorpost.

From the beginning, the Tower plans included many other buildings in an extensive campus surrounding a plaza – palaces large and small, temples of all flavors, shrines, markets, administrative buildings, schools, public gardens, supply depots, apartment complexes, livestock yards, and many other components of a growing population center.

The Tower was on a green belt next to the Babylon River, a man-made waterway that wrapped around the Central City, and it was enclosed by a double-walled defense perimeter.

After breaking ground on the project with a huge supply yard that also served as an inland port spanning both banks of the Great River south of the city, Nimrod had authorized the first structure in the complex be a small multi-faith temple. Ostensibly that was to placate workers by providing spiritual services to adherents of all gods, great and small. But few showed up to any of its events because they almost never got a day off.

Two years later, the temple was absorbed by Nanna International. In that case, it probably was prudent to focus on the moon god. The lunar calendar – and astrology in general – guided most of the schedule and design changes coming out of Nimrod's court.

Also, working with the Nanna organization was preferable to dealing with the Royal Diviners, who could throw any issue into turmoil by randomly tossing lots to make decisions.

By the time actual structural work began, most people had accepted the doctrine that the Tower should be a shrine to all deities, with ascending importance until you reached Marduk occupying the top floor. Everyone expected that certain gods would get special treatment over others.

Nanna was one of those favored by the masses, so the Lord Priestess was permitted to build an apartment home in the new complex – with an office, kitchen, servants, a storehouse, stables, and a private bed chamber.

***

Construction delays were common in most cases, but nobody had undertaken anything near this scope before. Unexpected issues popped up frequently. The most serious problem came when they discovered the water table was only 20 feet underground, due to being so close to the Great River.

Instead of digging narrow and deep to anchor the base, they had to change the design and dig wide and shallow. That added years to the project calendar.

In addition, the Tower was just the apex temple in a complex that supported more than 500 businesses and 50,000 workers. At its center was a massive plaza, bordered by the buildings.

Soon after Level One was finished, engineers discovered the long row of structures was funneling wind across the plaza into gusts reaching 50 miles per hour. Maintenance teams scrambled to build a series of ropes for pedestrians to hold so they would not get blown to the ground crossing the plaza.

The upside: While they were on-site, workers also added new benches, planters, food kiosks, and outdoor dining areas.

Details like that had filtered up from Babylon over the years, and some of it was interesting to Eber. However, after their tour five years earlier, life got so busy that anything related to the Tower slowly became occasional communiques from Azurad's family in the south. That allowed the couple to focus on building up their business and family without looking over their shoulders.

***

Eber had figured out early that expanding trade routes also could be leveraged for delivering information, so he paid his import and export partners extra to be communications carriers – often with bags of carefully stacked clay cuneiform tablets. Azurad and others in the community always appreciated the news from home, especially having left on less-than-ideal terms.

After being pressured by Nimrod to participate in the Tower, Eber met with his father-in-law alone and told him face-to-face he would not help with *any* part of the city.

Soon after, Azurad and Eber were called into a tense family meeting on short notice. Before anyone could speak, Azurad stepped forward and announced her family was moving north "to pursue exciting new business opportunities."

Nimrod was not fooled by the duck-and-run tactic, but he also clearly was not fully engaged in the conversation. He had more pressing things on his mind at the time, offered Azurad a courtesy hug, and asked what time dinner was being served.

Eber's family quickly excused themselves and did not stay to eat. Two days later, they loaded family, servants, and possessions onto wagons and camels. After a brief and polite farewell, the entourage headed north.

They were more relieved than sad.

***

Initially, the family moved to Ebla, a budding multi-national trade hub near the coast specializing in wool. The trip took almost three months, but they finally felt beyond Nimrod's reach.

They also adapted quickly. Azura and their sons loved the sea and rolling limestone coastal mountains. And since Ebla had developed a network of nearby agricultural settlements, Eber found reliable sources of grains to purchase for resale.

However, his long-term success meant he both cooperated with – and competed with – other traders at various times. That notoriety drew the attention of a growing band of pirates that cruised the eastern coast of the Great Sea looking to seize goods heading south.

One night about three years after the family moved to Ebla, an armed group of pirates rowed to shore from a vessel anchored in a cove, then hiked toward the town two days inland with the goal of killing Eber and stealing his inventory. But local militia volunteers detected the pirates and turned them back well short of the city.

One pirate was captured and gave local officials detailed information on their plans. Based on that, Eber and Azurad decided to move much further inland.

They had to relocate beyond the Great River, because pirates rarely crossed it. As the boundary of the "Land Between," just getting there was a hard five-day hike, and supplies had to be carried on carts pulled by oxen on well-traveled roads. Even if you avoided detection, once across the Great River your forces would be exposed – and most likely seriously outnumbered in a fight that far from your ship.

Just to be safe, Eber and Azurad moved all the way to Harran City, almost a month's walk from the coast – deep into the Land Between, past the Great River and up one of its major tributaries, the Balikh River, to its confluence with the Juliab River along the base of the northern mountains.

Harran was one of the early settlements in the First Sending, so they were welcomed by a large extended family – including Terah and his relatives, whose trip to Canaan had been put on indefinite hold when they settled in the north.

With Abram and Sarah in the area, the family also had other followers of the Creator they could socialize with.

Despite having some sense of security in Harran, Eber also began carrying an 18-inch sword strapped to his left thigh under his cloak, which he could deftly draw with his right hand and knew how to use in a fight.

As daughter of the king, Azurad eventually had to endure a welcome-to-town banquet put on by leaders of the Harran Temple Council, who had no interest in Eber but hung on his wife's every word. Eber was relieved to be out of the spotlight, and he had no qualms with melting into the shadows.

He especially enjoyed watching old men try make an impression on Azurad by wearing hammered gold ephods and huge helmets with horns. He wasn't jealous. It was all part of Harran's small-town feel.

Who is invisible now? Eber asked himself, laughing.

Harran prided itself on being cosmopolitan despite having a much smaller population than the southern cities. As a result, it welcomed a wide diversity of views and faiths – so many that an idol-maker who was promoted to a priest could make an exceptionally good income, and double-dip at that.

They charged for the statue, then they charged a second time to "bless" that statue into godhood. Maintenance agreements made it a profitable mix of products and services.

With so many temples in the area, priests with good reviews had more customers than they could handle. That included the Nanna temple in Harran, called "House of Joys." It was less audacious than most, so Eber and Azurad maintained a polite relationship with its leaders. Mostly that meant attending major temple banquets – until a surprise visit by the Lord Priestess.

When Azurad received an invitation to a private reception in Harran the following day, it did not include Eber. She read it to him, broke it in half, and said, "Want to attend a party?"

Eber looked at Azurad and said: "Only if I get the first dance with the En-Priestess."

Both laughed nervously. The prospect of Eber showing up unannounced was exhilarating and terrifying at the same time, so they spent a long time discussing what to wear to the event. It was a good thing, because neither had seen such extravagance in Harran. Over-the-top decorations would have looked normal in Babylon, but here they usually seemed brazenly out of place.

Eber and Azurad dressed in tailored white tunics over wrap-around skirts, cloaks with petal-shaped fringes, and thick round belts. They stood out in a room filled with bold and bright colors, custom-made full-length sewn silk dresses, embroidered shawls, and quilted coats with sleeves.

Azurad pointed to an elevated platform, where the Lord Priestess was hosting a reception line. Eber noticed a smug smile on his wife's face as she took his hand, led him up steps, and worked her way into the queue.

Within a few minutes, a palace guard approached Azurad and asked her to follow – alone. She took Eber's arm, glared at the soldier, and pulled her husband along.

The guard grimaced, shrugged, and led them to a private room with several high-quality imported couches. Soon the Lord Princess entered. She paused, scanned Eber with Azurad, chuckled, and sat down in a chair facing them.

"Welcome, in the name of Nanna," she said, bowing her head while keeping eye contact with the princess.

"Thank you for the invitation," Azurad said, politely bowing in kind. "The décor and refreshments are wonderful. Your staff should be commended."

A soft knock on the door was followed by a guard entering the room. He was leading Terah, who was wearing a royal ephod. Eber was not surprised to see his descendant at the event, since he was on the Harran Temple Council, but Eber had no idea why he was in the room for *this* meeting.

The Lord Princess began to talk about how important Eber's relatives were to the region in their roles as priests – not just their beautiful statues, which made gods approachable, but also their spiritual leadership in infusing those deities with divine attributes needed to ... well, be the gods people know and love.

Then she announced that Shelah was stepping back from ministry, and Terah was being promoted to Minister of Faiths. It was time for a new generation of priests.

***

Nahor had died in Ur, and Shelah was getting too old for some sacred rituals, so the mantle had been handed to Terah via a Sacred Marriage ceremony with the High Priestess in Babylon the previous month. Nimrod himself had approved the transition.

"I hope you realize how valuable Terah is to our community – and valuable in *tangible* ways," she said. "In fact, anyone who hinders his ability to get gods to our citizens when they need them ... well, they get a very strong reaction from this community."

She paused, looked at Azurad, and forced a smile. "It gets a strong reaction from our king, too."

Azurad stiffened, looked annoyed, and was about to speak when Eber stepped forward first.

"Good evening, Lord Priestess," Eber said, with a respectful bow of his head. "I trust you are well. I am pleased to hear my relatives have been valuable to you in ... how did you say it? ... *tangible* ways. I would love to hear some examples."

His wife took her own step forward and added: "Yes, I would love to hear more, too. I am especially interested in the problem you mentioned of getting gods to market."

Azurad smiled, then added before anyone could respond: "Of course, *any* revenue problem would be troubling to my father."

At the mention of Nimrod, the Lord Priestess sat up and put her hands on the arms of her chair, visibly nervous. She spotted a servant with a tray of food, signaled for an assistant to announce dinner, apologized for the interruption, promised to finish the conversation later, then led everyone into the banquet hall.

She left immediately after dessert.

***

Despite the small victory, Eber and Azurad knew any campaign to eliminate idol makers would be long and difficult with little chance of success, especially since Terah's influence clearly was expanding from his home base in Ur to Harran, with Babylon in the middle. The best solution again ended up a little distance, this time from the Omnist crowd.

After the temple event, Eber and Azurad moved their family and business office out of the city limits to a farm in the foothills south of Harran. Now Eber could work from home and more spend time with his wife and sons.

Also, traders could stay at their small guest house and no longer had to go through Harran to start and end trips. An atmosphere of hospitality permeated their home. On a regular basis they would host home worship services and a meal with followers of the Creator, including Abram and Sarah.

After a few months, they only needed to go into the city infrequently for supplies. Eventually they were no longer seen as a threat, and life settled down. Eber was grateful they had a safe and isolated place to raise families, make a decent living, and still stay in touch with contacts in the south.

Other than suffering through the cold winters and an occasional snow barrage, the family adjusted well to life near Harran. And once they gained the trust of long-time residents, they discovered a fiercely loyal support system.

Eber sighed as he thought about his friends back in Harran.

*I would trade a family gathering in Babylon for Mangar fishing on the Balikh any da*y, he thought. Instead, he fulfilled his duties as Azurad's husband and accompanied her. *Her father is king, after all.*

Azurad occasionally reminded Eber she was a princess in fun. Eber would bow deeply and pledge his undying fidelity. Then they would laugh together over wine, or Azurad would take his hand and lead him to their bedroom. Or both.

Eber enjoyed some of her playfulness while in Babylon during the Tower Dedication – at least until she was reunited with her family. He was amazed at the flurry of hugs, squeals of happiness, cries of infants, and excited talking from a dozen women at once.

He took the opportunity to slip out of the room and walk out on a veranda overlooking the Great River to the east. A cart pulled up on the street below, and two men got out. One paused and looked up. Eber's spirits immediately rose when he realized it was Arpa, and he skipped down the stairwell to the floor level, where he warmly greeted his grandfather.

After embracing Eber, his grandfather turned to the other man, who was dressed in high priest attire traditionally worn only in royal ceremonies.

"Terah, I believe you know my grandson, Eber," Arpa said.

"Of course, we met in Harran," Terah said. "Good to see you again, my father."

Eber remembered him, of course, just not his position in the family line. As they exchanged polite greetings, Eber started calculating precisely where Terah sat in their genealogy. That was not easy, because generations had been compressed in the early years of the New World.

Arpa was born two years after The Deluge, Shelah was born 30 years later, and Eber 35 years after that. All had lived more than 200 years, which meant nine generations were alive at the same time. Eber knew Azurad could rattle off the connections immediately. However, she was not in the room, so Eber began to work backward in his head.

Peleg had a son named Reu, who had a son named Serug, who had a son named Nahor, who had a son named Terah.

Eber did some quick calculating. That made Terah his *great-great-great* grandson. The fact Terah was a middle-aged man left Eber suddenly feeling all of 200 years old. Still, he smiled, said "of course I remember you," hugged the man, and shared greetings from relatives in Harran.

But Eber noticed Arpa was socially distanced from everyone else, and it was beginning to irritate him.

"Come with us and meet my family," Eber offered.

"We would love to do that," Terah said. "But first I have to make sure my statues arrived intact. It's my first time presenting in Babylon, and I am quite excited."

"I would love to see your work," Eber blurted out before noticing Arpa with his arms crossed and silent.

"Excellent," Terah said. "Why don't you come with us now?"

Arpa looked less than thrilled, but Eber agreed and followed Terah into a large room on the ground floor of the palace. When they entered, a large sign announced: "The Twelve Gods of Babylon." Eber felt a heavy weight on his heart before even seeing the statues.

***

Terah had crafted a large idol for each month of the year, and it became his crowning achievement as a high priest – prominently placed in the Seven Heavens Temple on the Tower's Level One plaza. That exhibit had been privately unveiled to Nimrod and other officials the previous month, to critical acclaim, according to Azurad's sources.

After that, Terah's reputation grew quickly via word of mouth. The quality of his shop was so highly respected that getting an apprenticeship became intensely competitive. And it was much more than an internship. As a journeyman under Terah, you immersed in the craft – living with his family in their house and studying in his legendary home workshop.

Students made idols crafted from wood, stone, clay, silver, and gold. Then they glazed each with various colors and patterns, and embedded jewels throughout.

People came from as far as Egypt to venerate idols made in the shop. Often, those pilgrims would say they experienced *ni* in the home's backyard shrine and would buy one of Terah's statues, helping the family to grow a thriving business.

The result was that whenever Terah unveiled a new project, you could expect a packed temple. "The Twelve Gods of Babylon" display was no exception. It also was exactly what the name said – a dozen statues of gods lining the wall.

Glancing down the row of idols, Eber was amazed at Terah's creativity. He already had covered the most important false gods of the pantheon in previous exhibits, so he invented 12 new gods and made them using wood and stone.

Terah also announced a plan to bring a meat and drink offering to a different god the first day of each month, calling it the "God of the Month" program. Those included random gods representing mountains, storms, seas, rivers, sex, music, wisdom, and more – plus a bonus composite piece near the entrance featuring the ancient Akkadian "Trinity."

Prominent on each wall was a sign: "ALL GODS FOR SALE."

Eber grimaced when he read it, and then he glanced at Arpa. His grandfather looked old, sad, and powerless at that moment. They followed Terah on a walking tour of the display, hearing his narrative but not really listening. When they got back to the lobby, Eber and Arpa excused themselves and found a corner table where they could talk in private.

Things were worse than Eber had suspected. Terah and his followers worshiped whatever god was trending at the town gates. They hired street vendors to sell replicas of famous idols, along with knockoffs of medallions and other trinkets you normally had to purchase in the temples.

Eventually Terah became intrigued with Nimrod and his Tower project, seeing it as his chance to become big-time. He even ramped up production in his shop to meet anticipated future demand. As a result, his family quickly grew wealthy and powerful – and also deeply enmeshed in the Tower culture.

Just when Eber was getting depressed at the state of future generations, Arpa changed the focus.

"I know it sounds bleak, but there is cause for hope, Eber," he said. "Abram has shown he is a true believer in the Living God. Let me give you an example.

"One day Abram walked into Terah's shop while he was gone, took a stick, broke all but one of his father's clay gods, and left the stick in the hand of the largest statue.

"When Terah returned, he demanded to know what had happened. Abram said he figured the gods had gotten into a fight, and the big god broke all the others with his stick."

Eber laughed out loud.

"The Lord has something special for that man," Arpa said, his face turning serious. "Abram is the seed of a new covenant with God, but he has a long and hard road ahead."

"I fear we do, too," Eber said.

"More than you know," his grandfather said.

***

Arpa began to share what was happening behind the scenes at the Tower. In the early years, a relentless drought and heat wave had caused major delays and construction failures. In the final years, Nimrod put increasing pressure on managers to finish the project. Upper-level interiors were especially problematic, due to long time delays in transporting materials up a NimWay that was deeply rutted from heavy traffic.

Though Nimrod's fanatical focus on urban build-up had provided new economic opportunities for people, drawing many from rural farms to the cities, the local supply of workers quickly became insufficient. That forced contractors to recruit help from as far away as Canaan and Egypt. Many did not speak *Adamic*, so communication became increasingly difficult.

In the end, Nimrod just went out one spring with his army and pressured a few nearby city-states to provide slave labor to finish the job. He was especially harsh on men with dark skin, lashing out with a longstanding bigotry he figured was justified because of how he had been treated as a boy.

Autocracy and festering resentment eventually took a severe toll – on workers and on timelines as the ranks thinned.

If the resulting poverty, hunger, infant mortality, and rampant violence were not enough, prejudice against followers of the Creator became oppressive. It was led by the Nanna community.

Two years earlier, the organization had pressured officials in Ur to exclude the Sons of Noah from its "Festival of Faiths." Believers in one god were labeled intolerant and judgmental, a sentiment that had gained momentum in recent years.

"It isn't safe to be a person of faith openly in Babylon, so make sure you stay alert and watch your back while here for the Dedication," Arpa said. They stood up when Azurad approached.

"I have good news," she said.

"We could use it," Eber said.

"We get to see my brother, Eliezer" she said.

Azurad excitedly told how an old friend of Rasu had kept her informed of her younger brother's condition over the years, and Eber's grandmother had arranged for a meeting at the prison while they were in Babylon. The visit had to be short, but Azurad was grateful for anything after not seeing her brother for so long.

Just before dawn the next day, a woman came to their room and led them to the street, where they took a cart to a featureless, windowless building along the river southeast of the city.

It had high walls, men in battle armor patrolling the perimeter, and a smell so rancid they had to pull scarves over their faces to avoid retching.

Conditions inside were deplorable. People were emaciated. Many were injured but continued to work threshing and winnowing grain under threat of death. They represented a potpourri of ages, ethnicities, and social status. But all shared one feature – their eyes seemed vacant and defeated.

Excrement was piled against the fence, and Eber wondered how humans could treat others this way.

Guards led them into a small side room and told them to wait. Neither knew what to expect. The last time they saw Eliezer, he had been a strapping young man ready to take on the world. When the door opened, a much different person entered.

Eliezer was subdued, thin, and filthy. He also looked much older than his age. It did not matter to Azurad, who gasped, sobbed, and ran to embrace her brother. Eber soon joined.

The rest of the visit was a blur, as the siblings shared 10 years of life in 10 minutes. But one thing was clear: This was a changed man. He finally motioned to a table and sat opposite them.

"We only have a few minutes, so please let me speak," Eliezer said as they sat. "Do not feel sorry for me, sister."

Eliezer leaned forward and took Azurad's hands.

"God sent me here, not a king," he said. "All my life I longed to be a warrior. I thought that meant being like our father. The Lord brought me here to learn a different way. In God's kingdom, to be strong you must become weak. To be lifted up you must be brought low. And to be great you first must become a servant.

"It may look like I went from prince to pauper, but the truth is just the opposite."

A guard burst through the door and interrupted. "Visit is over," he said with a firm matter-of-fact tone.

Eliezer knew that meant *now*, so he said, "I love you," stood up, hugged his sister, touched foreheads with Eber, and followed the guard out – waddling in ankle chains. Azurad and Eber watched them go through an iron gate with a lock and into a courtyard with other prisoners.

"Eber!" said Azurad, pointing to her brother.

Eliezer had walked through the crowd of prisoners to the back wall and was leaning against it. The Companion was standing next to him.

8

Early Warning

Special events like festivals, birthdays, anniversaries, and dedications seemed redundant to Eber. After the first 100 years or so, they usually rolled past him – unless they caught the attention of Azurad. The Jubilee celebration for the Tower's 10th anniversary was one they could not avoid attending.

After a decade, nothing about the trip to Babylon seemed the same, starting with the road itself, now almost impassible from heavy usage. Even rivers were clogged with barge traffic. Also, irrigation and navigational canals siphoned water from the Great Riven on regular intervals from Sippar all the way to Ur.

More people also meant more crime. Small bands of armed robbers roamed throughout the region, especially at night, so security was a much higher priority this trip. In addition, they had to be concerned about a growing population of aggressive animal predators, including lions and bears.

We hunted them, so they started hunting us, Eber thought.

Arpa had told stories about how the relationship between humans and animals eroded from the moment they walked off the Ark together. He joked it probably did not help that the first thing Noah did after leaving the Ark was kill some of them as a sacrifice to God – after saving them from The Deluge.

The first generation of the Wilds struggled to adapt and survive after a year of being caged, fed, and socialized by Noah's family. The fittest left the Ark and instinctively headed down the mountain, eventually making their way along a stream that joined a small river. Occasionally the family had to follow ridge lines above, but humans and animals seemed content to stay near the main group heading downhill until they reached open highlands.

The second generation of animals was different. They put up with people because their parents did, but they began to withdraw from human camps as hunting moved from obtaining food to field sport. The animals seemed to sense it was no longer just for survival, but rather for recreation. The concept was so foreign, the animals pulled away further.

The third generation was the pivot. Many never acclimated to humans. The first serious case was when a son of Jephthah was severely bitten by a 5-year-old Grey Wolf he had raised from a cub. It culminated, of course, when Nimrod and his spear holder were mauled to death in a hunting accident decades later.

***

Because of the increased risks on this trip, Eber arranged for his family and personal guards to join a large group of traders, who brought defense dogs and armed security teams.

Eber had trained dogs early in his life and always came to love them, but after going through 10 pets he decided the emotional investment was not worth the frequent sense of loss.

Eber had never needed guards before anyway. He could handle himself. Besides, over many years of traveling for business, he learned his best weapon was disciplined awareness. True, he had been the best grappler among his brothers and was competent with a sword, but at his age there was the issue of being ... well, *older* than most. That just heightened his vigilance.

When the Tower finally came into view and the crowds thickened, Eber's anxiety finally faded.

The City of Babylon was an immense grid of open squares, straight and broad boulevards, and narrow and winding lanes that spiraled out to large flat plains. Built across both sides of the Great River, its steep embankments made the city a fortress as well as a flood control system.

The walls of Babylon were 300 feet high, 85 feet thick, and measured a day's walk on each side. The outer wall was surrounded by a wide and deep moat. With numerous security checkpoints, it took almost five days to traverse the entire city.

A smaller wall ran parallel inside, with an enclosed space between them. Also, where the main wall met the Great River, a return-wall ran along its bank that doubled as a rampart. A lower River Gate for ferry and barge traffic could be closed for defense.

Contractors were instructed by Nimrod to build security into everything, and it became a big draw for families moving to Babylon. Streets ending at the river were guarded with gates and armed guards, but the tightest security was at main buildings in the city's two central sectors – the Royal District with the king's two palaces, and the Sacred District with the Tower at its heart.

The "New City" West Side and "Old City" East Side were connected by a fixed bridge more than 1,000 feet long and 30 feet wide. Nimrod's magnificent Royal Palace stood at the east end of the bridge, and it was virtually impenetrable.

The Royal Palace was a mini city of its own, second only to the Tower as an architectural wonder. It was defended by three concentric walls – an outer wall half a day around, a middle wall slightly shorter, and an inner wall adorned with colorful bricks and murals of hunting scenes.

Those paintings frequently depicted Nimrod hunting big cats, such as leopards and tigers.

The northeastern Summer Palace was smaller and less posh, with a single wall around it. However, it was favored by younger family members who loved to play games on the broad, sloping grass parkway around it.

Over the years, Babylon continued to develop at a much faster pace than the rest of the world. In part that was due to raised riverbanks that protected city residents from seasonal floods that previously left the valley an inland sea.

With most basic needs met, the region quickly became famous for its ability to generate scientific advancement. Thinkers moved from physical sciences such as astronomy and biology to internal logic systems and philosophy, where a few even declared that all gods were dead. What started as a scientific revolution quickly became a revolt against God, and the Tower was its banner.

Still, after 10 years and no showdown with a heavenly army, the Tower shifted from being a statement against God to being a statement for humans – and the center of global culture. Many said it had ushered in a new Awakening among humans.

However, near the end of the 10th anniversary celebration, Eber was having trouble just staying awake. He was exhausted from the whirlwind week of lavish ceremonies, concerts, art exhibits, awards, dedications, and endless banquets.

Long ago Eber had realized he was an introvert at heart, so he was happiest if he could just sit in the background and disappear. It usually worked, for a while.

***

The day before the main anniversary celebration, which was to be capped by a swanky invitation-only evening reception and lodging on Eden Plaza, Azurad's family hosted a brunch at Nimrod's Summer Palace. In her family, "brunch" meant a feast with lots of food, beer, more food, and more beer.

As a favor to his daughter, Nimrod agreed to let his youngest son out of prison long enough to join them, though it was just for the one meal.

Azurad was determined to have a restrained greeting with Eliezer, since her father was watching closely. But when she saw her brother at the door, she could not contain her joy, ran to him, and jumped into his arms. Eliezer was still thin, but he looked strong, clear-eyed, and unintimidated.

In a crowd of expensive purple and red attire, he stood out in a simple prison tunic – and did not seem to mind. Eliezer slowly walked up to Nimrod's table, bowed deeply, and thanked his father for allowing him to attend.

"I figured you could use a good meal," Nimrod said while chewing on a leg of grilled gazelle. "We have the best roast duck in my kingdom."

"Thank you very much, my lord, but I only eat vegetables now," Eliezer said.

Nimrod looked puzzled, shook his head and chuckled.

"That's fine because it just means more meat for the rest of us," he said. Nimrod got an unexpected awkward silence from his guests, so he scanned faces until people started laughing. When it settled, he stared at his son.

"I hope you have learned more lessons than how to eat beans," Nimrod said.

Eliezer's face softened, and he placed his hands on his heart.

"I have learned much, my father," he said. "Most important, I discovered my life purpose."

Nimrod put down a pheasant breast, half-wiped his hands, then laughed dismissively.

"What could you possibly find behind bars?" he asked.

Eliezer smiled and said softly: "Him."

Nimrod's countenance changed in an instant. He became angry, tossed aside his napkin, and stood up so fast he bumped the table and knocked over several glasses of wine.

"I said no talk about religion today," he said. "Now go back to your table and out of my face. Or go back to your cell."

Azurad started to protest. But she saw the determined look on her father's face, bowed, and gracefully backed away, pulling Eliezer by his belt. Eber followed.

They got to the back of the room just in time to see Terah and Abram walking toward the head table – the final two in the royal reception line. Eber remembered asking God how it could get any worse. Then it did.

Terah bowed deeply and greeted Nimrod. But Abram stood with his hands clasped behind his back, staring at the ceiling. After a few uncomfortable moments, Terah nudged Abram. He did not move.

"Forgive my son, my lord," Terah said sheepishly. "He is a troubled young man, but he does truly respect and honor you."

"Really?" asked Nimrod. "What part of his failure to bow or greet the king is respectful?"

Abram stepped in front of his father and said, "The part where that king claims to be god."

Nimrod began to rise, looked around the room, saw people had stopped eating to watch his reaction, then sat back down and leaned forward.

"Is there a god stronger than me in this room?" Nimrod asked, pointing to a row of statues along the wall.

"There is only one *real* God here, sir," Abram said.

"Ah, so you're a One-God advocate," Nimrod said. "And which one is that?"

"The one who created all things," Abram said.

"Tell your God we have created plenty of gods and temples to suit our needs," Nimrod replied with disdain. "In fact, in the main lobby we have a large number of bronze and clay deities you can touch, worship, and even buy. I hear some are on sale."

Nimrod looked at the crowd, and people laughed nervously. But Abram stood erect with his walking stick, set his jaw, took a step forward, and said:

"There is only one Creator, king Nimrod. And if you do not remove false gods from your kingdom, he has the power to destroy it all – starting with your Tower."

Nimrod rose from his seat enraged, and the entire room stood along with him.

"I will show you who has power," he shouted. "Should throw you in my furnace? Would that prove I am your God?"

Eber began to hyperventilate. Everyone had heard stories about Nimrod's huge furnace, ostensibly used to make large quantities of burnt bricks but also rumored to be a convenient way to incinerate the insolent.

Instead of cowering at the thought, Abram smiled, bowed respectfully, and said nothing.

Nimrod grew increasingly angry with the silence until he finally motioned for the captain of his Palace Guard. Eber took a deep breath, then started to step forward to plead for Abram's life. But Azurad cut in front of him and boldly walked to the front of the king's table, where she put both hands on the tabletop and looked Nimrod in the eye.

"Oh father, if you truly think this man deserves punishment, why kill him now and be done with the justice?" Azurad asked. "Wouldn't you rather make him suffer for a long time?"

Woah. Eber did not see that coming, and he began to sweat. Nimrod looked surprised, too, then broke into a broad smile.

"Interesting thought, daughter. What do you propose?" he asked. "But mark my words, I want his entire family punished every day for the rest of their lives."

"My king, you can have your wish," she said. "Banish them to a place where they will just be voices in a wilderness, separated from their homeland for life with no one to hear their ramblings or pleas for mercy.

"Exile them to Canaan. It is the territory of our descendants from Ham, where they will be foreigners and no threat."

***

Nimrod, whose attention was fading by the minute, signaled a passing servant for another beer, then turned back. "Just get them out of my world," he said gruffly.

"Thank you, my father," she said. Azurad bowed deeply, turned, immediately herded the men to the door, and pushed them through. Then she paused at the door frame and turned.

"Oh, my father, if you would indulge me on one more thing," she said. "As you said, my brother Eliezer also has been an irritation to you. Send him away with the Chaldeans, and you will never have to deal with any of them again."

Nimrod clearly was feeling the effects of the alcohol and was having trouble forming the right words, so he simply waved his hands and grunted.

Azurad was out the door before he took his next sip. Eber was waiting at the street. They quickly put Terah, Abram, and Eliezer on a cart heading out of the city – though they had to coax Terah, who was having trouble processing the notion he was facing *de facto* exile when it should have been his finest hour. At that moment, Eber only cared about one thing.

"Are you OK?" he asked his wife.

"I'm fine," she said. "I'm just relieved to be past that. Can we just go to the party tomorrow night and have some fun with my family before we leave? I doubt my father will wake up from his nap until it's over anyway."

***

When Eber and Azurad arrived at Eden Plaza the next afternoon, a lively celebration already was in full swing. Children had been excluded, so food and wine mixed freely with music and adult conversation. And lots of laughter.

As expected, Nimrod was sleeping off yesterday's beer and probably would show up after midnight. That was no problem. His cohorts expected it and were getting the party started for him – or at least getting *themselves* started.

Since the event was hosted by The Marduk Group, about an hour into the program everyone was asked to sit for a few awards to be presented. After several inside jokes Eber did not understand but most of the crowd did, the emcee gave out cuneiform certificates of appreciation for work on the Tower.

After about an hour, Azurad moved her chair toward Eber, leaned over and laid her head on his shoulder. He began to worry she would fall asleep and snore.

Then a "keynote" speaker got up. He was a young, energetic priest of Marduk – wearing a modern take on the ephod that featured an imprint of a rainbow made with dyes. The man bounded around the stage energetically, encouraging people to stand up and clap.

At least it got Azurad to wake up, Eber thought.

The speaker settled into a 15-minute lecture titled: "Imhullu and You." Eber was mildly interested, because the "Imhullu" had fascinated him as a boy.

Simply put, it was a powerful and divine "evil wind" that was the main weapon of Marduk. Since he was Babylon's patron god, his primary implement of war had been of much interest to participants in Shelah's discussions.

The Imhullu had grown in importance until it became part of the Pantheon story of creation. In the most common version, Marduk used his divine wind to defeat the water goddess Tiamat in a titanic primordial battle of the gods.

"Marduk used the seven winds to defeat his enemies," the priest said. "Let me share with you how those seven principles work in our lives today."

Eber groaned internally. He knew that meant parsing out each of the seven "winds" of Marduk as teaching points. Still, he had enjoyed the stories as a youth.

Shelah often regaled children with details on how the sun god had trapped the water goddess with the four winds, then defeated her with three extra winds – the Imhullu, a whirlwind, and a cyclone. In the end, Marduk entangled Tiamat with her own net, then filled her with Imhullu until he could finish her off with an arrow to the heart.

Applause signaled the speech was over, though Eber could recall little of the content. During an obligatory hour standing next to the king's daughter in a reception line, Eber spotted his grandfather sitting at a table next to a support column, motioning them to join. Once there, Eber and Azurad finally had some privacy and could talk.

After eating dinner and getting off their feet, everyone started to feel better. Arpa asked how the brunch had gone, but when he saw the look on Azurad's face, he changed the subject.

"I haven't heard anyone talk about Imhullu in a long time," Arpa said. "My father said the Creator would eventually mock false gods by turning their own weapons of war against them. If true, maybe Marduk will be brought down by his own evil wind."

Eber turned to ask what Shem had meant, but a clay jar with a candle crashed to the floor near them, spilling flaming wax on a carpet. Servants quickly put out the fire, the commotion settled, and the room got quiet.

Then Eber heard a strange sound, like the Great River roaring at flood stage, and the entire building began to vibrate.

***

Without warning, a wall of strong wind tore across the terrace from east to west, ripping the patchwork hide sunroof from its stands and slamming it into a row of tables filled with people. Some were knocked over the edge of the wall. Many people dove to the ground but were being hurt by flying furniture and pottery. Eber and Azurad rose to their feet, glanced at each other, and started to cross the room. But a second gust blew both to the ground, hard.

Eber scanned what was happening around him. People were bleeding and crying for help, but the wind was too fierce for him to stand and it was continuing to build. He noticed the temple room at the base of the Needle was intact, with its west-facing door flapping open and shut. Its main walls were extra thick to support the Needle and looked to be holding up under the wind.

"Let's get people into the temple," Eber shouted. Azurad glanced at the building, looked back, and nodded. They crawled to a nearby group huddled under tables and directed them to the building. Peleg and Joktan were standing at the door waiting to assist, having already carried Arpa and Rasu into the building.

Some attendees had escaped down the Stairway after the first blast, and about 30 people huddled together in the block building. Some were being tended for injuries. Others began to pray for the wind to stop, but it only picked up. The building was being buffeted with debris driven by something akin to a typhoon. Eber prayed the building would hold up.

Then a banging noise began inside the Needle, louder each time it struck. Soon it was clear that whatever was making the noise in the Needle would break the building apart if it continued.

Eber was never sure why he acted on instinct next, but it saved lives. He stood, ran to the back of the room, and opened the small door leading into the Needle itself. Then he closed the door behind him and locked it, ignoring Azurad pounding on the door. Eber looked up and saw the problem.

A long wood ladder led to a trap door at the top. Its hatch was attached by a rope to a pulley system on the floor, and the entire mechanism had broken free at the bottom. The trap door was banging open and shut in the wind, swinging its 100-pound iron pulley around like it was being held by a Nephilim.

For a moment, Eber was unsure what to do. His mind recalled images from his dream, and this was too close for comfort. Then he thought about the fact his wife was in danger *right now*, took a deep breath, and started climbing up the ladder with a cloak pulled over his head to ward off rubble blowing down the shaft.

At the top, Eber could see flashes of lightning and swirling sand through the hatch. He reached up to close the door. Then he saw the Companion standing in the middle of the platform.

He was surrounded by a phenomenon that Eber could only describe as an invisible wall blocking the fury. Large angels with swords stood on either side of the Companion, while a vortex of debris clouds and hard rain swirled around them, held back by ... well, something not natural.

Without thinking, Eber climbed through the hatch and closed the door behind him. He turned to see more, but the Companion had his hand up.

"Take off your sandals, Eber," he said. "This is holy ground."

Eber slipped off his sandals and fell face-down on the platform. Soon he felt strong hands on either side lift him to his feet, but when he looked up the angels were gone. The Companion was gazing out at the raging storm.

"God has seen what people are doing in the guise of reaching him," he said. "They even kill each other in his name. The Tower is just a symbol of the problem. People believe they can force their way to God's rewards.

"Their arrogance is an offense to the Lord, and he will tolerate it no longer. The Creator will bring this Tower down with its own symbol of strength – wind. Take your family and flee *now*."

Eber dropped to his knees, with a storm of emotions raging inside now. The faces of his wife, sons, and grandchildren came to mind. Eber began to sob.

"Oh Lord, please spare my family," he cried out. "It would take us a full day just to get out of the Tower. You delayed your wrath for Noah. Please hold back your anger for us, too."

The Companion turned to Eber and nodded. Rasu had often talked about how God was merciful and usually gave clear early warnings of coming punishment. In the case of Noah, it had come more than a century in advance.

Standing on top of the tower, Eber would have settled for enough time to evacuate his family. He got more.

"For the sake of your family, God will delay his justice," the Companion said. "But he *will* bring down this Tower with a holy wind. The hour is set. It is one year from today. All who hear and ignore your warning will perish."

***

The wind stopped instantly, and the vortex encircling them dissipated quickly. Eber glanced up to see sunlight breaking through the clouds. He looked back and found he was alone – and still much higher than his anxiety would allow – so Eber carefully climbed back down the ladder, unlocked the building's door, walked through the temple, and entered a terrace in chaos.

Tables were overturned, people were crying in pain, and multiple fires were burning. Three men were battling the worst fire, which had been ignited by an overturned oil lamp that splashed onto curtains. Eber went to help, scanning the room for his family as he walked.

He saw Azurad wrapping cloth around a woman's bleeding leg and was relieved his wife appeared to be uninjured. She looked up, made eye contact, and paused. Something profound had happened to her husband on the roof, and she noticed it in his countenance.

As Azurad scanned Eber's face, her frown faded into a look between puzzled and knowing. Then she cocked her head, smiled grimly, nodded, and turned back to tend the injured woman.

9

The Destruction

Approaching the ridge atop the Cliffs of Najaf, Eber knew the Tower was about to come into view, but he hoped it was gone. Tomorrow was the Day of Destruction. At least, that was what his family had been calling it since his prediction 12 months ago.

Everything about the past year had been driven by Eber's encounter with supernatural forces on the Tower during the First Wind, and it had kept him up most nights since.

Lord, I would not mind if this were just another dream, he prayed. *Just please wake me when it is over.*

The cart did that for him when it bounced on a rock and yanked his attention back to the Ridge Route. The crest was just ahead, so the road had turned from packed river sediment to chunks of limestone. The cart stopped when a wheel was blocked by a large rock, and the leader tried to coax the ox team forward.

Despite her age, Azurad was not one to wait for an ox to decide the next step. She sat up, looked at Eber, adjusted her belt, checked her blade, scooted to the edge of the cart, and hopped off. The entire family piled out behind her and followed her up the hill. Eber sat alone in the wagon for a moment, took a breath, got off, and followed at a distance deep in thought.

After the events on top of the Needle one year ago, nothing had been the same. Eber had gone through the motions of life with little energy. When Azurad tried to get him to talk about it, he just looked at her with vacant eyes and shook his head.

During their two-month return trip to Harran from Babylon, Eber fell into a deep depression, with frequent sadness and night terrors for no apparent reason. He rejected all offers to discuss it, which left his family frustrated.

At first, he convinced himself he was hesitating because nobody would believe him; but deep down he knew it was because they *would* believe him. Once that happened, his world would change. He would have to carry a heavy weight of accountability, especially with such specific details, including a date.

This was Eber's moment of truth. He was relieved it was finally here yet apprehensive about possibly being wrong. Or horribly right.

Doubts had crept into his mind before he even got home from the First Wind, but Eber could not deny what he had seen and heard that night. One morning, he fell on all-fours and cried out to God for help. While deep in prayer and weeping, he felt strong hands on his shoulders, but when he looked up, he was alone.

For some reason, after that Eber felt enough courage of conviction to share with his wife what had happened at the Tower – though he did wait until the last week of their trip back to Harran. Azurad was immediately supportive, but she also had questions Eber simply could not answer.

A few weeks after they returned to Harran, Azurad finally opened up about her doubts over what was happening – and whether she really believed Eber. On a walk, both were deep in thought and silent when she stopped and turned to face him.

"I need to know you are absolutely certain you really saw and heard those things on the Tower," she said. "Are you sure it wasn't a dream, like when you were 15?"

The comment seemed glib to Eber, which immediately made him defensive, so he turned to confront her. Azurad could see she had hurt his feelings and quickly said, "I'm not mocking you, my love. I just need to know how real it *really* was."

Eber started to reply harshly but paused when he noticed his wife's face. He had never seen Azurad so frightened. And why not? If this event happened, her family in Babylon could be facing life-or-death struggles. Eber's compassion for his wife rose above the perceived affront, so he took her hands and offered the only reassurance he could.

"I encountered a real, physical manifestation of God's power, my love, and its purpose was to issue a clear warning," Eber said. "I am a businessman, not a religious expert. I cannot explain the spiritual universe or why he picked me, but I cannot deny seeing those things with my eyes and hearing them with my ears.

"Beyond that, I am as terrified as you are about what that prophecy means."

Next it was Azurad's turn to soften. She squeezed his hand and said, "That is good enough for me, my love." She never questioned him again.

***

Despite reservations from family and friends that grew as the Day approached, Azurad pulled together a team to issue warning communications. She started by enlisting their sons and close relatives in an awareness campaign, sending out a barrage of cuneiform communiques to Babylon using Eber's courier connections. Those messages alerted family, friends, community officials, faith leaders, and many others to a possible building structural issue.

It was an imposing communications challenge, with the highest of stakes. Eber first tried delivering the warning to his family using truth – a story that included angels and a mystical wind wall – but not many people believed in things like that anymore. In addition, the religion of the God of Noah was viewed as being obsolete and abusive by many in Nimrod's hierarchy.

Because of that, Peleg had suggested they frame the Tower warning as a brick integrity issue. He figured people might be willing to work off-site for a month while "upgrades" to fix a credible problem were installed. He even provided a list of alternative work sites.

A few people took it seriously, but most saw it as over-reacting to an unlikely event – a freak wind incident from the east, when the prevailing winds were from the west via the Great Sea. Worse, neither he nor Azurad had seen the Companion since returning to Harran months earlier.

Where is he when I need him most? Eber wondered. *And when I need to hear him clearly, why is he silent? Nobody trained me for this. I am grain trader, not a priest.*

The grind of continual rejection and misgivings left Eber wondering what he really *had* seen and heard that night. He finally shared his concerns with Azurad in their garden one afternoon, but it quickly shifted to Eber complaining about God choosing someone as poorly prepared as him for such a monumental task.

Azurad listened patiently for a while, then looked up at Eber and said: "If you think God should have picked someone more qualified, you are in good company. My grandmother told me Noah used to say the same thing."

She stood up, shook the dirt off her apron, kissed Eber on the cheek, and displayed a self-satisfied smile. Then she walked out of the garden with her basket.

***

That exchange was a rare moment of levity in a year of overwhelming heaviness. Eber became more intense in every area, especially at work. His son Joktan already had expanded their product mix by adding crops such as chickpeas, beans, lentils, apples, and pears. Eber built on that by leveraging their Great River network to move timber directly from the mountains to the southern cities.

During that year, Eber also invested deeply in a group expanding the Steppe Route, an ancient overland trail stretching from Damascus to the far southeast. In recent years, The Steppe had been leveraged to transport new types of trade commodities such as silk, horses, furs, beadwork, musical instruments, and precious stones. The possibilities seemed unlimited.

Though business kept him occupied, memories of angels holding back a storm on top of the Tower kept rising to the surface. He simply could not escape the weight of fate: A collapse of the Tower would have devastating consequences, including destruction of the city and the death of thousands.

Also, in the initial weeks after the First Wind, he had blurted out specific details that were under scrutiny now – especially the exact day the Tower would fall. When Nanna International got wind of the predictions of doom coming from Harran, they responded by scheduling a major festival at the Tower that week.

The Lord Priestess had confiscated one of the warning tablets from Harran and confronted Peleg about its content. At the time, he was working in Mari designing a new type of raised canal off the Great River. The Lord Priestess learned Peleg was there, so she traveled from Babylon to Mari on "temple business." While there, she hosted a luncheon and invited Peleg. After being introduced, she wasted no time getting to the point.

"I've been wanting to meet the son of Eber," she said. "Your father is one of those old-school holdouts who still believes there is only one god."

Then the Lord Priestess gestured toward a long row of idols lining the wall of the hallway. "I prefer not to limit myself," she said. "Each god brings value on its own, and many of our people will testify these gods bring real benefits. Why wouldn't you believe in them?"

Peleg said, "With all due respect, Lord Priestess, I *do* believe in every one of these gods." He pointed to them and broke into a grin. "I just don't believe any of them are *real*."

The Lord Priestess started to reply, hesitated, and stood.

"Just be careful, Peleg," she said. "Holding an unpopular social position these days can be harmful to your business – and your family's safety, which I'm sure is your primary concern."

Before Peleg could ask if that had been a threat, she motioned for a scribe.

"Perhaps our time would be better served on something less ethereal," she said. "I suggest infrastructure repairs."

Peleg figured shifting topics was a sensible idea at that point, but their face-to-face meeting still ended up being a long and tedious series of acrimonious disagreements.

Though Peleg was diplomatic, he was not intimidated. He had earned widespread respect and status as a superb leader who took the time to learn local languages and customs when doing business. Nobody was more experienced in negotiating deals, especially contracts with temples for canal upgrades.

However, when the Lord Priestess threatened to destroy his family by invoking a curse from Nanna near the end of a long and hot day, Peleg responded in a way he *somewhat* regretted later:

"I'm not worried about any curses coming from the moon." Peleg said. "The Creator made that, too."

***

The Lord Priestess then loudly offered specific ways she could hurt the family if he did not stop spreading rumors. Unfortunately, Peleg had little to offer in rebuttal beyond a prophecy from his father. Worse, it was in the name of a religion she saw as archaic and patriarchal.

And she was not the only one who felt that way.

Attendance at God of Noah services had fallen to fringe status, and anything before The Deluge now was considered myth by most people, so few in Babylon were receptive when Eber's family warned their deity was going to destroy the biggest and best building of all time. Open minds usually ended at "God" in the conversation. Still, members of the small but mighty "Eber Crew" did all they could to save lives. The rest was up to God.

Family members discussed at length whether to witness the event, but the debate ended when Eber said he was attending, no matter what the outcome. Though he had not chosen this path, he would see it through.

Peleg suggested a spot that would be a safe distance away from the Tower. Najaf City was perfectly located – two days southwest of Babylon, on a high plateau overlooking the Great River valley below. Also, the city was an ancient settlement, with elders who had grown up knowing Arpa, so its people were warmly hospitable to his family.

Eber was glad they had traveled from Harran instead of Ur. The trip to Najaf was easier from the north because you could come up the gradual slope of the Najaf-Karbala Fan. Walking uphill for two straight days was no fun but coming from Ur was tougher. You had to ascend steeply from the Great River by traversing the ridge on the back side of the cliffs overlooking the Najaf Sea. That stretch usually left lungs and legs burning.

I do not miss those switchbacks, Eber thought.

As he paused to look down on Babylon and the Tower, the only thing that seemed to have changed in the past year was *more* ... of *everything*. More people, traffic, livestock, boats, roads, artificial waterways, and especially more buildings fanning out from the city walls on the plains to the west.

Anxiety began to build in Eber as he thought about the innocent ones in the potential path of destruction. His hands got cold and clammy, but Azurad took one in her hands and leaned against him.

"You did all you could, love," she said. "Let's find a place to pitch our tent, clean up, and eat some food. We'll feel better then."

Eber started to say something but knew she was right, so he just nodded his head and motioned for her to lead. Focusing on tasks always helped to mitigate their stress.

A grove of trees by a small spring under a shutter ridge offered firewood and some protection from the elements, so they set up camp overlooking the city and Tower. They were an hour northwest of Najaf City, where the rest of the family was staying, because Eber wanted to be at the viewing point Peleg had identified by dawn. That meant pitching a tent nearby.

As the sun set over the high desert to the west, Eber felt caught between two dreadful futures – tomorrow either nothing would happen and he would be labeled a false prophet, or the Tower would fall and devastate countless lives. He could think of no third option.

***

A sky full of stars greeted Eber as he stepped out of his tent on the Day of Destruction. He had gotten little sleep, so once the eastern sky had a hint of reddish light he decided to stop tossing on his mat and get up.

The gentle, cool breeze was refreshing, and it sharpened his senses. The air was clear, nature was quiet, and everyone else was still asleep. Eber knew that would not last and wanted to take advantage of the solitude, so he spent an hour alone praying. He got no answers yet again, so he got up, went back to camp, and volunteered to help with breakfast chores.

In mid-morning, Eber heard a group coming up the trail. Peleg rounded a bend leading his wife, children, and a few friends. Azurad was the first to greet them, scooping up her grandchildren and leading her flock to a table set with grapes, licorice, dates, and other treats. It was followed by greetings, hugs, and news from the south.

Eber motioned for Peleg to join him sitting on a flat mesa with an unfettered view of the entire valley looking north and east. They made small talk about the trip while frequently glancing at the city below. Babylon was the crown jewel of Nimrod's kingdom, and the Tower was its most visible symbol.

At that moment, Eber just wished it had never been built.

It almost wasn't. After winning popular support for the Tower early, Nimrod hit a snag when he approached local officials.

They were concerned about the environmental impact of the construction and influx of new people. However, in a stroke of genius, Nimrod pitched it as an historic urban renewal project – a city within the "City of Cities."

The Tower complex would house numerous buildings for administrative and religious use. And it would have a world-class amphitheater to host concerts with top artists performing for large crowds. All would be funded by taxes.

Babylon officials loved the idea of replacing their poorest neighborhoods with an economic powerhouse. They agreed to tear out a large section of the East Side inner city, called "Oxbow Row" because of its many metal-working shops.

The area was a haven for imported workers who had lost their jobs when the first Marduk temple was finished. However, nobody would stand up for the immigrants against Nimrod's land grab, so approval by the City Elders was unanimous and the shops were forced to relocate to other parts of the city. They tried to appeal to the Royal Court, but it refused to hear the case.

Eber often wondered why someone needed that much land for one building, until he saw it up-close the day of their tour. To hold the weight of a building that tall, Peleg said the base had to be wider than it was high. That meant in the end it looked more like a mountain than a tower.

Layered construction theory was relatively simple – a series of increasingly smaller square platforms laid on top of each other. By making each level smaller the farther it got from the ground, engineers could design ways to distribute loads enough to support the sheer weight of the whole.

Each level was constructed separately, with a core of sun-baked mud bricks covered by a layer of fire-baked bricks, glazed in different colors based on astrological importance. Step-up walls were masked by rich ornamentation and offered large outdoor terrace spaces.

Ceremonial bricks were engraved and sold as paid sponsorships, with cornerstone positions especially popular – and expensive. A layer of bitumen was used to glue the burnt bricks in place and to protect the core from rain. In addition, the outer walls were dotted with holes to release excess moister.

The top levels included staggered setbacks to fit in more apartments with terraces, which fetched a premium.

A penthouse with a terrace was reserved for royalty, celebrities, and the very wealthy. Looking out at the expansive view from the top later, Eber understood why they charged so much. The Level Ten terrace, with its 360-degree view for 100 miles, was always a must-see site for tourists and pilgrims coming to Babylon. It just took a century to deliver.

Will you really destroy it in one day? Eber asked God.

***

Looking down at the Tower, he could think of no earthly way a structure that mammoth could blow down in a wind. Fortunately, he was distracted from his anxious thoughts by the squeals of children running amok behind him.

A large group was coming down the trail. It was Joktan leading an ox cart filled with his wife, 13 rowdy sons, and a surprise guest – Eber's grandfather.

The family had urged Arpa not to make the trip at his age, but here he was bouncing on the back of a wagon. Arpa had firmly insisted on coming, so Joktan insisted on making the trip happen. One of his business partners brought Arpa to Najaf City, where Joktan had picked him up.

Eber hugely appreciated his son at that moment.

The next 30 minutes became a cacophony of conversations, hugs, and laughter. Eber spent a long time watching his grandfather from the fringes, soaking in memories. Then he stepped forward, everyone else stepped back to watch, and Eber embraced his grandfather. Both were in tears. So was everyone.

"A Day of Days," Arpa said after a few minutes. Eber was too emotional to respond and just nodded. He had not expected so much support, and it left him humbled.

With the flurry of activity now settled, women took over and set out food and drinks on flat rocks overlooking the valley. The family spent the next few hours eating and drinking together, catching up on life, tracking children, and discussing Nimrod's latest venture in Nineveh. Nobody wanted to bring up the Tower.

"What's that, grandpa?" Reu asked as the sun was waning.

Eber turned to see Peleg's oldest son pointing toward the Zagros Mountains on the east edge of the Land Between. Clouds seemed to be rolling over the mountains like waves, flowing onto the plains, then building in height and speeding up as they moved due west. The whole family stood to watch.

It soon became clear the cloud was really a lot of *things* being pushed by a powerful Easterly – a stew of sand, wood, rocks, and debris of all kinds driven by an extremely strong wind from the east. They had seen major sandstorms coming from the desert before, but nothing like this.

The storm quickly grew into a thick wall 1,000 feet tall and five miles wide barreling toward the city. Azurad moaned, then gathered the children into a circle, surrounded by the women.

The family watched in horror as the growing wave of destruction seemed to assimilate everything in its path. Entire farms disappeared in the cloud, with only barren ground left behind. Tornadoes were spinning on either side of the wall, which accelerated as it crossed the Shinar plain. Eber gasped out loud when he realized Babylon was directly in its path.

First, the wind hit the walls of the city. Those were enveloped by the cloud, where the east-facing walls disintegrated into a huge ball of detritus, now roaring toward the west at 200 mph. Eber reached for Azurad, who was reaching for him.

Next, the wind hit the Tower with the force of two typhoons. The main impact struck Level Six and took out the operations team immediately. Those first responders had been positioned above any conceivable flood level, but "wind from God" was not in their disaster recovery plan. Today they were just trying to survive themselves.

For about 10 minutes, the bottom third of the Tower disappeared from view as the cloud enveloped it. When it moved past, they could see the tempest had obliterated most of the city. It almost reached Karbala before the wind died and the wall of *things* simply dispersed.

Through breaks in the lingering dust clouds, the family could see large chunks missing from the lower-level terraces, but the Tower was still standing.

Eber's mind was a jumble of confusion, wondering if he should be happy or sad the structure was intact. *Maybe it was a symbolic judgment,* he thought.

Peleg asked if anyone could see the Summer Palace, where Azurad's family was staying. That sparked a hum of conversation, until someone shouted, "Fire!"

Thick smoke was coming from the windows on the west side of Level Six. That was an immediate concern. After the First Wind, Peleg had warned people about fire danger. With so much reliance on lamps and candles, he felt a major incident could gut the inside of the building even if the structure remained standing.

Soon smoke was coming from Level Seven, too. Then fire began to flow out in streams from windows on all the upper floors. For hours, the smoke and fire grew, while the city around it seemed to be a mass of flattened buildings and conflagrations. The sun was starting to set when Eber wondered if this was God's end for the prophecy – and his dream.

"No way," Peleg said.

Eber turned to see the Needle on Level Ten suddenly drop until its top was barely visible, then stop. The entire building shuddered and made a groaning sound they could hear from their location. After a few seconds, the tip of the Needle disappeared from their view, followed by a large amount of smoke and debris blasting out of the windows one level below, Level Nine. A few minutes later, the same thing happened on Level Eight. Then Level Seven.

"The floors are collapsing on top of each other from the top," Peleg said.

Fire had so eroded supporting infrastructure that everything on Level Ten had crashed onto the floor below. Soon the impact and additional weight caused that floor to fail and fall on the level below. The Tower was crashing internally, floor-by-floor. When all nine interior floors hit the ground at once, the building shook but remained intact for a few moments. Eber thought maybe the outer structure would survive.

Then Joktan said, “I think the Tower is leaning.”

Suddenly, an enormous explosion blew out windows and walls around the entire bottom floor, causing the Level Two floor above to drop in a crush-up phase. One-by-one, the outer walls collapsed onto the missing level below it until the Needle crashed onto Seven Heavens Plaza.

Finally, the entire Tower crumbled into a large cloud of combustible dust, which exploded out for miles into fires that burned for weeks. In addition, heavy debris demolished nearby buildings – especially the impoverished areas to the west.

While Eber was trying to process the devastation below, he noticed the wind had become light and variable. It was over. The only sound was quiet sobbing.

The family had come to support Eber, but most had seriously wondered how any wind could bring down Nimrod’s man-made mountain. Now they knew. Their response was a mix of fear, awe, gratitude, and concern.

***

Few in their group got any sleep that night. They knew many people would need help, including Azurad’s family in the city.

So early the next morning they held a brief family meeting, packed up their gear, and headed down the hill.

Joktan and his family were assigned to take Arpa back to Ur, where they would remain to assist with the expected flood of refugees heading south – at least until it was safe to return to Harran in a few months.

Azurad would lead a team into the city to find her family and friends. Peleg needed a closer assessment before deciding his direction, so his family joined Eber and Azurad traveling north down the Fan Road to the Karbala Gap.

After saying farewell to the group heading south, Azurad simply turned and started walking without another a word. Eber and five volunteers from Najaf City were right behind.

As they rounded a small rise and approached a long straight stretch of path, Eber saw the Companion setting a brisk pace far ahead of them.

10

The Confusion

The acrid smell of molten bitumen forced Eber to pull his scarf over his face as his family approached the Karbala Gap, two days after the Day of Destruction.

Vast fields of cereal grains had extended from here to the western city wall, but now they were piles of smoldering embers. Chunks of brick and steaming globs of black goo were scattered everywhere, including on the road.

The family stopped to discuss the situation. First, this was no place for children, so Peleg and his wife decided to take their sons – plus two orphans they found abandoned along the road – to Sippar City, one day north along the river. Since Azurad knew Babylon much better than anyone in the group, she was the logical choice to lead a team into the city to find her family.

They agreed to rendezvous at the Gap in three weeks, and Peleg's family headed toward the Great Ridge.

When they were out of view, Azurad looked at her husband, tightened her belt, set her jaw, put her head down, and started walking east toward Babylon – with Eber and the five men from Najaf trying to keep up.

As the team wove through what was left of West Babylon Village, cries of pain seemed to come from everywhere. Most of the entire area west of the city had been reduced to a relentless mass of rubble, with vague pathways where roads had been. They appeared to be the only ones wanting to go into the city, but the line of people trying to flee was longer than they could see.

Azurad finally got frustrated with the mass of refugees, veered onto a side street, and led her group through a featureless maze of demolished mud-brick homes with families huddled around fires outside makeshift tents. Any structure still standing looked like its bricks had been scrubbed clean of everything, including paint, by wind-blown sand.

The sun was fading by the time they approached the Royal Gate – the main entrance to the double-walled City of Babylon from the west. Azurad told the men to wait for a few minutes, then she disappeared. An hour later, she returned with two women she obviously knew.

"These women served in the palace when I was young, and they used to bring me to the river to play," she said. "They had shown me where they lived, so I was able to find them. They said the city is too dangerous at night right now. We should wait and go to the Tower zone at first light."

It made sense. However, it also meant Eber, Azurad, and the men from Najaf had to spend a restless night laying on mats in a fallow field, trying to sleep with the mournful wailing of children and adults in the background.

Early the next morning, they surveyed the main city from the west. It looked worse in the light. Also, getting through the western gate and outer wall would be just the first step.

Most of Azurad's family was at Nimrod's Summer Palace. That meant they had to enter the city, navigate what remained of Babylon's West Side, cross the Great River, find a way through the East Side, get to the palace in the northeast quadrant, locate her family, and make sure all were safe.

No problem, Eber thought.

He was contemplating a strategy when Azurad started walking. He grumbled to himself and followed.

Having grown up in Babylon, Azurad knew the many side routes – especially hidden paths running between the walls. That would be key now, because the Second Wind had pulverized the east and west walls with direct hits, but it left the other four outer and inner walls mostly intact, offering safer routes to the palace.

When they reached Babylon's western edge, the Royal Gate was mostly intact. However, just outside the city wall, hundreds of people were burying loved ones in makeshift graveyards – carefully crafting small mounds to cover the corpse, adding offerings to "monsters" and a small amount of food for the departed's journey.

Eber lamented at how quickly things had changed. Many of the mourners in that field would have sought expensive burials at Dilmun, because it reminded people of The Garden. Now everyone was getting a pauper's grave.

Azurad pushed through the crowd, pressed through the gate, immediately turned left, hugged the wall, and waited for the others to catch up. Eber saw the pandemonium in the streets and realized how difficult a task they faced.

***

Babylon was a vast city that sprawled out across both sides of the Great River. Its walls formed a hexagonal pattern – with the river running through the heart of the city and multiple canals cutting across both sides for fresh water and transportation. Eber was exhausted just from getting to the main entrance, yet they still had a long way to go.

Azurad paused and gathered the six men against the wall just inside the city gate.

"My friends said to avoid the main Processional Way through the city," she said. "They told us to follow the wall north to the corner tower. From there, we head northeast and stay between the walls all the way to the river. Once there, we can take the river path south to the bridge and cross over."

It was good advice. Later they heard the central areas on both sides of the Great River had devolved into anarchy, with riots, looting, little security, and piles of dead bodies just outside the Tower disaster area. The wall path was quieter, and the few people they passed were going the opposite direction with heads down. The gate at the northwest corner was blocked by large chunks of debris, so crowds were thin there, too.

From that point on, they were the only ones on the path.

When the team reached the river, Azurad led them down to a rarely used trail near the waterline, which they followed south all the way to the bridge. They scrambled up the embankment and looked across the river.

The East Side was in shambles. Until a few days ago, only the most wealthy and prestigious people could afford to live on this side. Even a one-bedroom apartment in the Temple Complex was priced too high for palace service workers, who had to live across the river and walk for hours to get to work. Now *everyone* was being forced out of the city.

Fortunately, the only bridge across the Great River had survived, but it was severely damaged. An agile young man from Najaf led them across single file and roped together, sidestepping the many holes and piles of hot bitumen.

***

On the east bank of the bridge, they walked into mass confusion. Hundreds of people were milling around the main entrance to the inner wall. Many had strips of charred skin hanging off their arms and legs, with clothes blackened by smoke and blood.

The "Gate of the Gods" was just a scorched arched tunnel with broken hinges and no doors. A lone bureaucrat vainly tried to calm people in the plaza, but an angry mob shouted him down.

Azurad took advantage of the chaos. She pointed left, took the lead again, and pushed through the crowd along the wall parallel to the river until they came to the Temple of Marduk. Azurad opened a small door behind the temple, which led to a space between the inner wall and the temple's back wall. It had a narrow path she had used since childhood.

Though the temple was in shambles, most debris had blown over the river and into West Side neighborhoods. That meant they had a path around the worst of the damaged East Side.

Eber was relieved to be out of the crowds and making progress. Most of Azurad's family lived in the Summer Palace near the city's northeast corner, so they followed the river wall that direction.

Through a damaged section of the barrier, they could see the Northern Fortress on their side of the river ahead. It had been reduced to its mud-brick foundation. The Southern Fortress across the river now was just one corner tower sticking out of a debris pile that included crushed ferry boats.

Azurad led them through a door into a what used to be a vast greenbelt, with a path leading up a hill toward the Summer Palace. Now it was littered with trash and smoking pieces of various materials.

They searched around and through the palace for hours, but the building was heavily damaged and abandoned. Finally, Azurad sat down on the front steps and began to cry. Eber sat next to her, put his arm around her shoulders, pulled her close, and started to speak when he saw someone about 100 yards down the hill from them.

It was the Companion. He was standing next to a shrine that was almost invisible because it had been dug into the hill below the palace and was surrounded by a grove of trees.

Eber said, "Azurad!" Before she could respond, Eber was on his feet jogging down the hill. When Azurad saw the Companion, she followed – and ran past Eber halfway there.

The Companion led them around an orchard to the front of the small temple, where they found servants standing guard outside. Azurad greeted them, but they replied in a language nobody could understand. Exasperated, she turned to the Companion for help, but he was gone.

The servants gestured for her to follow and led her into one of the few shrines in the area that had been built with stone blocks. When they opened the inner door, 20 members of Azurad's family poured out to hugs and tears.

Eber exhaled deeply. *Finally, some good news*, he thought. Then he noticed the shrine was dedicated to "The Unknown God." *They know him now*, he thought.

The irony almost made Eber laugh, but right now he needed to help tend people who were seriously injured, so he found his wife and served as her runner for supplies over the ensuing week. Things did not go smoothly because they were having trouble communicating with the servants who had saved so many lives.

And nobody knew why.

***

A*damic*, once the sole human language, long ago had been deemed a boutique dialect to study for historical value. Eber remembered the first time he had heard another language, at a trade conference when a descendant of Japheth attended with a representative from the far Southeast. Now Eber's family was the only one who kept it as their core language.

That decision felt short-sighted as Eber tried to communicate with the Palace staff. They missed Peleg's linguistic skills, but Azurad found a way to communicate despite the obstacles. She spoke a little Sumerian and her family's nurse spoke some *Adamic*, so they were able to piece together what was happening.

As expected, news was not good. The family had been able to get to the protected shelter in time thanks to an early warning from a sentry in the northeast palace tower, who died saving their lives. But most of their friends and staff had been killed – many crushed when buildings were flattened – or were missing.

The billowing cloud of black dirt, silicon, and even trees had transformed grating into spears and fences into arrows.

Of course, the biggest toll was at the Tower itself, where almost 3,000 were feared dead. Nimrod's Palace Guard had quickly shifted from locating survivors to body recovery. Burns and lacerations from sharp flying objects left most people nearby seriously injured. Fortunately, there were many acts of heroism in the crisis, too.

A breakthrough came when the palace physician turned Nimrod's banquet hall into a large makeshift hospital, including long rows of mats with people needing intensive care. Finally, there was hope, but it was not for the squeamish.

Helpers were scraping bitumen off skin, amputating limbs, wrapping open wounds, applying salves, cleaning up blood, and pulling sheets over the dead.

Eber and Azurad were not trained medical staff, so they volunteered to help at the front door, checking people into the center and comforting where they could. At first, they treated injuries such as broken bones. But that quickly shifted to people who were getting diseases from the poor sanitation conditions.

The third day, a wagon pulled up with a stretcher, and soldiers carried it into the hospital.

"This is our Miracle Lady," the driver said as he got off the wagon. "She was discovered alive at the northern edge of the Tower wreckage. We never expected to find any more survivors, but this one most definitely has a will to live."

They took her into a side room, where the doctors could treat her in private, since her injuries were so severe. Azurad slipped inside, then came out to report.

"It looks like an older unnamed woman," she said. "They found her under an archway in the rubble near the Tower – about an hour after city officials announced they had given up hope of finding anyone alive. Her face is burned beyond recognition, and she is in awfully bad shape."

A familiar wind began to flow between them. They looked at each other, stood up, and turned in tandem.

The Companion was sitting next to the bed of the new patient. Without thinking, Eber walked directly to him and stopped. He suddenly was not sure what to say, so he pulled up a chair to face the Companion and sat down. Azurad watched from the door.

A soft moan from the woman drew Eber's attention. She was in critical condition. Her skin had open blisters over much of her body from fires. One arm was crushed. Her left ankle was dislocated. A blast of liquid bitumen had blinded her. She was coughing blood. And her clothes had been virtually burned away.

While waiting for a doctor, Eber covered the woman with a blanket. Then he took a damp cloth and gently cleaned her face. If she was important to the Companion, Eber wanted to know why. Over the next few hours, he never left her side. Though she lay unconscious, he talked to her while touching her good arm – assuring her she was not alone.

At one point she opened her eyes and turned her head toward Eber's voice. Without thinking, he began to sing a simple melody from his childhood called "The Rainbow Promise," a song passed down through Noah's family. Eber's grandmother would sing it to calm the children during thunderstorms and earthquakes:

The Rainbow Promise

When storms approach, He warns ahead
In waters deep, He lifts our head
On mountains high, He takes our hand
For the Rainbow Promise forever stands
Yes, the Rainbow Promise forever stands

Eber stopped singing after about 10 minutes, when the woman appeared to be sleeping. He quietly got up and left to find Azurad. She was getting ready to leave for some rest, so Eber asked if she was OK with him staying, just until the woman was out of the woods.

"Of course, my love," she said. "That is why we are here. Be safe, and don't stay up all night – again."

Azurad kissed Eber good-bye, turned to leave, took a step, turned back, kissed him again with more intent, smiled, and left for the wine cellar. Cots were set up there for hospital workers to get some sleep. It was one of the few quiet and undamaged spots in the palace.

Eber headed back to the "Critical Care" room. The Palace Physician was waiting for him at the door. He said the woman probably would not make it through the night. Eber was confused by the news and just stood silent for a few moments.

Deep in his heart, he had been expecting a miraculous recovery to validate his efforts. Instead, it seemed like God was just being cruel. Eber shook his head and walked back into the hospital. The woman was sitting up.

"Feeling better?" he asked.

"No," she replied honestly. "But I am alive – for now."

She coughed blood into a cloth. Eber handed her some water, and she drank deeply.

"What was that song you were singing?" she asked.

The question took Eber by surprise, because he had assumed she was asleep.

"Just a folk song of hope from my childhood," he said.

"No, it's a song about the God of Noah," she replied.

Eber froze. As he stared at her face, recognition began to form. Then it sharpened into focus – and it was an unexpected reality his mind had trouble accepting.

"Lord Priestess, I'm so sorry. I should have recognized you," Eber said. "Please accept my deepest apology. Is there anything you need?"

She knew he was taking the high road and followed his lead.

"No thank you, Eber," she said. "I do remember *you*, and your son Peleg. Not the best of memories, mind you, but certainly better than today."

She forced a chuckle, and Eber awkwardly followed suite. He was struck by her resolve in the face of such complete devastation.

The Lord Priestess had been leaving the Tower when the wind hit. She was sheltered by a retaining wall until it collapsed on her, trapping her in an air pocket under a stone arch.

"I thought long and hard about my definition of 'god' while lying there helpless," she said.

***

For the next two hours, Eber and the Lord Priestess talked about faith, their families, how they got into their respective careers, favorite festivals, musicians they loved, and mundane aspects of life they would miss.

Just before midnight, the Lord Priestess gasped in pain and asked to lie back. Eber helped her, then sat next to her in silence.

"Do you really believe there is only one god?" she asked after a few minutes. "How can you really know for sure?"

Eber was not expecting that. He offered a short silent prayer to God for help, then he leaned forward.

"I'm not a religious professional like you," he said, "All I can tell you is what I have seen and experienced first-hand."

The Lord Priestess coughed violently, so Eber paused, helped her sit up, gave her some water, and helped her lay back down. Then she motioned for him to continue.

"My father was a priest and idol-maker, so I was exposed to many different gods and religions from an early age," Eber said. "Most temples were communities of everyday people just trying to find purpose in life. Over the years, I met a lot of temple leaders with high morals doing compassionate things.

"But I only found one real God." Eber hesitated.

"And he wants to be found by *you*, too. He has been waiting to restore his relationship with you all along."

Instead of objecting, the Lord Priestess sat up, her face softened, and tears began to stream down her face.

"After all I have done, God would still want a relationship with *me*?" she asked.

Eber wished he had exactly the right words, so he paused. Then he smiled and softly sang, several times:

"On the Mountain of Mercy, He takes your hand,
For the Rainbow Promise forever stands."

As he sang, the expression of her face slowly morphed from surprise to confusion to denial to astonishment to pure joy. Then Eber realized she was no longer looking at him. Instead, she was focused on something over his shoulder.

Before he could turn around, he felt the strong presence of the Companion. Eber turned to see him smiling at the Lord

Priestess. And she was smiling back at him. When Eber realized what was happening, he was astonished into silence.

Soon after, the woman drifted into a peaceful nap, so Eber walked out into the hall to get some fresh air and bumped into Azurad – pretty much the last person he had expected to see at that hour. She had not been able to sleep, and *something* told her to come back upstairs.

Eber took a deep breath and told his wife what had happened – and that the woman inside was the Lord Priestess.

Azurad looked startled, then angry, then seriously *focused.* When Eber started to speak again, she motioned for him to stop, shook her head, turned, walked into the room, and went directly to the bed of the Lord Priestess.

Eber knew better than to follow. He watched his wife sit in a chair next to the bed, lean back, fold her arms, and begin to talk. A glance toward Eber told him to stop staring, so he left the room.

When Eber checked in later, his wife was leaning forward and looking at the Lord Priestess, who was laying on her side facing Azurad. They were deep in conversation, so Eber slipped out again. When he returned, his wife had moved her chair close to the bed and was holding the other woman's hands. Both were crying, so Eber left yet again to give them privacy.

About an hour later, Azurad came out in the hallway wiping her eyes. She looked up at him, started to speak, then just buried her face in his chest and wept.

After holding his wife for a few minutes, Eber led her to a place where she could clean up. Then they returned to the Critical Ward and sat down on opposite sides of the Lord Priestess. She smiled, closed her eyes, sighed, and fell asleep. For the next two hours, they held her hand in silence while the Companion watched from the end of the bed. Words were not necessary.

Late that night, the woman's breathing became labored, and she began to gasp for air. Eventually the Lord Priestess exhaled her final breath. Eber sat there hoping to hear her revive, but after a few minutes he put his head in his hands and started to sob.

He felt an arm drape around his shoulders. It was Azurad, who also was crying. Suddenly, she stopped and gasped out loud.

Eber sat up and followed her finger pointing out the window. The Companion was walking down a path toward the east into the sun, which was just starting to emerge from behind the mountains. He was helping someone who looked like the Lord Priestess, and she was still wearing a blood-stained blanket around her shoulders.

Every few steps, she seemed to get stronger, until they melted into the glare of the sunrise.

11

THE DISPERSAL

Eber felt only emptiness as he walked through the Royal Gate heading west toward the Karbala Gap. After three weeks of assisting people who were devastated and often near death, the seven who had left Najaf now shuffled forward in single file on a steady uphill hike – silent, exhausted, covered with soot, and deflated by the massive scope of human need in Babylon.

The sight of Peleg and his family waving from a ridge above boosted their spirits. Azurad kneeled to greet the children racing toward her, then stood to embrace her son for a long time. Eber realized he had never been so happy to see Peleg, so he instinctively wrapped his arms around both his wife and son.

When Eber turned to survey the valley below, he sighed. Though fewer fires were burning, the mountain of debris would take decades to clean up. And the loss of life was incalculable.

"It took a hundred years to build it, and one day to bring it down," Peleg said in a matter-of-fact tone. Then he shared what they had learned at Sippar.

The city was spared major damage from the windstorm, but the flood of refugees fleeing north along the Great River was staggering. The roadside was littered with abandoned household items, human excrement, and corpses. From what he had heard, the road heading south toward Ur was at least that bad.

"I'm assuming Babylon is the worst," Peleg said. After an awkward pause, Eber realized Azurad was just staring at the ground, so he stepped in.

"It's bad everywhere right now, my son," Eber said.

Then he described the suffering they saw – especially during the first two weeks. Nimrod had arrived from Nineveh quickly, with a "Babylon Rising" tour of the city that briefly raised hopes the government would help. Even Azurad had been persuaded to join the tour to boost morale in her hometown, but mostly Nimrod just shook a lot of hands and pledged to rebuild better than before.

However, he returned to Nineveh the next week.

In the end, Nimrod decided that building over the "Mountain of Misery" would be more trouble than it was worth. Within a year, he announced a new series of cities in the north – and promptly moved his Royal Palace to Calah, leaving others to pick up the pieces.

***

Fixing a broken city was the easy part; healing broken people was almost impossible. Thousands of lives had been torn apart in body, mind, and spirit. Worse, nobody knew what to expect going forward – or if there ever would be a return to "normal" life.

During one tour, Eber and Azurad had a chance to see the main tent city, in what had been the amphitheater. They also toured food banks, feeding tents, a makeshift orphanage, and field hospitals that were so overwhelmed they placed mats on the floors of gift shops.

At one point, Azurad visited a group of children who had lost arms and legs, but she became overwhelmed by sorrow, excused herself, walked outside, sat on the steps, and wept so intensely she began to convulse. Eber followed her out and tried to console her, but she stopped him, looked up with tears flowing down her face, and asked the question nobody could answer but God:

"Why the *children*?"

No answers came, and no Companion appeared.

Azurad stood crying for several minutes, then faced Eber. He wrapped her close in a bear hug, kissed her neck, and then just held her. After a few minutes, she pulled away and blew her nose in a cloth handkerchief.

"If you're asking why, my love, no words suffice," Eber said.

"I know," she said. "But I also believe this – God cares deeply when his children suffer. I feel it. And I have seen it in action."

Then Azurad wiped her face with a scarf, tightened her belt, grabbed his hand, glanced around, and led him out the door still sniffling. She took him through a series of bustling back streets to a large tent filled with the poorest of the poor in the city. Most of the people there had lost relatives, friends, houses, businesses, schools, temples, and faith.

They had no families, no jobs, no homes, no food, no god, and no hope.

When Eber entered the tent, he expected to find despair inside. Instead, people were laughing, singing, eating, and serving those who could not help themselves. A novice harp player tried in vain to lead a song, which just added to the approachable potpourri of activity.

Then Eber saw the Companion. He was standing next to a group of women serving food behind a table. They were impressively busy while chatting joyfully about their grandchildren. Eber felt Azurad come up from behind and lean against him.

"I can't explain why or how, but he shows up in hard times," Azurad said.

Eber looked at her and smiled. "Maybe in hard times, we show up for him," he said.

They both laughed, and then just stood enjoying watching people be kind to each other. The Companion was smiling broadly and tapping his foot to the beat of the song.

On their way back to the palace, Azurad took a detour to thank the servants who had saved her family. She softly knocked on the door of a one-level house that was damaged but intact. A short, rotund, and jovial man opened it and greeted her – with a respectful bow for the princess. Azurad returned the courtesy, then she laughed and hugged him warmly.

Inside, about 15 people were sitting where they could. It was a home worship and study session for followers of the God of Noah. The Companion was sitting in the middle of them.

Eber was surprised. He thought the One God movement had fallen apart as a formal religion after only one generation. By the time Arpa was having children, his relatives already were making up their own gods – controllable deities they could touch, see, and use to meet their needs. To honor their grand idols, they built majestic temples, including the Tower.

Azurad's grandmother said God preferred more intimate settings. Lavish ceremonies with large audiences were not the model Noah's family had followed. The Creator had commanded humans to disperse, so believers met in small groups instead of large buildings.

In fact, followers of the Creator had *never* built a temple to their God. Though that small-group format did not attract large numbers, it also did not collapse with the Tower. And they were not locked into a specific building to seek help or comfort from their God in a crisis.

The group leader told how several of the large temples in Babylon had tried to maintain status quo – continuing to hold meetings in their damaged buildings. However, some early attempts met with disaster, most notably when fractured beams collapsed and killed 15 priests of Marduk rehearsing for their first public service since the Second Wind.

Nimrod did not want any more deaths on his hands, so he ordered all religious activities to be suspended. That led to a confrontation with Nanna International, which said the king had overstepped his authority.

Religious leaders came together and called for a "Separation of Temple and Kingdom" mandate. Nimrod simply ordered the arrest of anyone who disagreed.

In the end, his stay-at-home order forced *all* faiths to meet in small groups around the city.

City officials made one final attempt to convince people their old lifestyles could be resurrected by scheduling an outdoors concert on a makeshift "New Seven Heavens Plaza." Top musicians from various temples offered to participate – if they had survived. Unfortunately, the concert was repeatedly postponed because of poor air quality from ongoing fires and slow progress of clean-up efforts.

The city eventually gave up on a large-scale event and produced a small acoustic concert at a venue near the river and the Summer Palace – for invited guests only. It was lightly attended and never repeated.

***

N*obody is concerned about politics or music right now*, Eber thought as he stood at the Karbala Gap looking down on Babylon burning. All the posturing by Nimrod and his minions seemed trivial at that moment.

"People are facing great hardship, and many have given up hope," Azurad said as she hugged Peleg's wife, Lomna. "There are so many displaced people, and so few resources."

Then she stepped back, surveyed her family, put her hands on her hips, and said: "But we are not a people without hope. God is with us, as he was with Noah and Emzara.

"The world may have crumbled, but we have a real God who warned us so we could save our family. Does anyone think he will fail us now?"

I love that woman, Eber thought.

His wife had fully matured into the role of family matriarch, and he hugely appreciated having such a strong partner in those hard years after the Tower collapsed. Standing at the Karbala Gap three weeks after the disaster, Eber needed all the counsel he could get, because he knew the decisions his family had to make would affect future generations.

Since Peleg lived in Ur, it made sense for him to return south and consult with Arpa on next steps. With the ongoing exodus from cities, a Second Sending seemed to be already in progress and inevitable. Ignoring it was out of the question at this point.

"We can either manage this migration process, or it will manage us," Peleg said. "We need the Sons of Noah to agree on a division of land again, or we will lose it all."

That meant an historic second dispersal. Since Arpa was on the Council of the Sons of Noah, he could spearhead efforts with the other two sides of the family. Peleg would work with the elders in the south and get word to his parents, who would return to Harran and wait for Joktan's family there.

The Sons of Noah quickly agreed to set up the Council headquarters in Erech, the first city built by Nimrod, about 60 miles northeast of Ur. The challenges they faced were immense and urgent.

Most significant was the inexplicable breakdown in communication, which hindered every step they tried to take. It got so bad in Babylon that the city was pejoratively called "Confusion City," or "Babel."

***

Years ago, Arpa had talked about how humans often let the pace of innovation get ahead of their ability to understand it. The incessant drive to do more, build higher, and think deeper meant change often outpaced wisdom. Consequences were not important. And nobody knew what anybody else was doing, because everybody was stuck in communication silos.

Peleg called it the "Babel Dilemma," where unfettered progress caused breakdowns. In the early days of the Tower, engineers wanted their own terminology and acronyms, more out of boredom than necessity. Soon, everyone also wanted their own professional language – and wanted theirs to be the standard – on top of their native languages.

Near the end of construction, Peleg estimated that people from 72 ethnic groups were working on the Tower at one time, and few could understand terms used by other departments. Fewer could speak *Adamic*.

It came to a head five years before completion when workers threatened to strike unless they could use their original languages on the job. Nimrod's supervisors were forced to capitulate. However, the resulting need for translators proved to be disastrous when the Tower collapsed.

Most interpreters working at the Tower site were listed as dead or missing after the Day of Destruction. A few survived, but they left to check on their families and homes. With no translators on-site, rescue and clean-up teams had no way to understand each other. Many additional lives were lost as a result.

God was forcing humans from their cities into a distributed world, for a second time. And it seemed to be for their good, again. The Creator understood the many risks of people bunching in high-density populations – from poverty and food scarcity to lack of sanitation and diseases.

People just keep repeating the same mistakes generation after generation, Eber thought.

He hated to sound pessimistic, but the tendency to rebel against God seemed consistent. And it went back to The Garden. Yet for some reason, the Creator still seemed determined to restore order.

Clearly the next step was a Second Sending.

Standing at the junction near the Karbala Gap, Eber knew his son faced a huge task, so the family gathered to pray. Then they departed three directions – Peleg and his family heading south to Ur, the men from Najaf returning southwest up the Najaf-Karbala Fan, and Eber and Azurad traveling north to Harran.

A few months later, Joktan and his family returned with news from Ur. Arpa had called a meeting of the Elders Council to hear Peleg's report. The surprise attendee was Shem, who had traveled four months to support his son and family. Arpa had not seen his father in more than 100 years, so their reunion was quite emotional. In fact, when Arpa recounted the story later, it was one of the few times Eber saw his grandfather cry.

About a month later, all the participants had arrived and were rested. After days of discussion, the Council made the key decision to appoint Peleg as Dispersal Director.

"Peleg is the perfect choice – and not just because he's my boy," Azurad said proudly.

However, everyone knew the challenges were formidable – especially in *how* the allocations would be determined. It would be difficult to assign specific territory to families and not show even an appearance of favoritism. At one point in the discussions, Peleg asked for a few days off "to contemplate the issue." Then he disappeared for a week with Shem.

***

When Peleg returned, he asked Arpa to assemble the Council. He and Shem had gone to Arpa's cottage south of the city to discuss options. The unexpected move was brilliant and visionary. Shem was still held in high esteem as son of Noah, so his counsel had significant weight on the decision.

Also, Peleg figured God had given Noah the model he wanted, so why re-invent the wheel? Since an eyewitness was still alive, he figured it was worth learning more.

"The Creator wants this done by casting lots," Peleg told the Council. "It was his original model, cannot be accused of favoritism, and we need a speedy solution that will satisfy all families. I started with a list of places our families went in the First Sending. Those areas already have settlements, and I suggest we grandfather those into the allotments, so they stay within their families.

"Otherwise, we will follow same general flow of movement – with Shem's family in the Land Between, Japheth's descendants moving to the Lands Beyond the Seas, and Ham's tribe migrating into the Land of the Nile. We will cast lots for sub-divisions."

The Council had little choice but to agree, since people already were on the move.

The biggest issue was the land of Canaan. In the First Sending, Ham's son had been allotted territory to the far northwest near the Great Sea. Instead, he went south of that area and occupied Shem's land from Lebanon to the River of Egypt.

Canaan's entire family was upset with his decision. Ham, Cush, and his brothers urged him to reconsider. However, Noah was angry and loud, because all involved had taken an oath to abide by how the lots had fallen by chance.

"You settled in a land that is not yours and did not fall to you by lot," Noah said in a confrontational family meeting. "If you do this, you and your sons will be cursed with continual strife and rebellion. You will reap what you sow. Take the land by sedition, and you will fall by sedition. You and your children."

The issue grew so big, Shem moved near the City of Salem to support his family, which had rightly earned the land when the lot fell to them. Noah soon followed, and they settled into a rural existence in the northwest hills of Canaan, where there was abundant grazing land for their sheep and livestock.

Unfortunately, the area again was an issue in the Second Sending. Some argued it should be grandfathered in like other areas, but others said that would just reward Canaan's descendants for illegally seizing Shem's land in the first place.

The debate became so heated in Council meetings that Peleg became concerned it would derail negotiations. Then in a stroke of desperation more than inspiration, he proposed deferring a decision on Canaan for 100 years. With few other options, the Council quickly OK'd the "Canaan Compromise."

After announcing their approval, Arpa and the other elders commended Peleg for his work, sanctioned his approach, told him they appreciated his respect for Shem, prayed over him, and sent him off to do the work.

As Peleg was leaving the room, he turned, and bowed deeply.

"My fathers," he said, "if you would indulge me one personal request before I leave. Each of your families gave rise to nations, each with their own languages. But the Second Sending will isolate us further and may render us unable to communicate.

"I humbly ask that you allow the family of my father, Eber, to keep *Adamic* as its core tongue. Then if the other families maintain *Adamic* as a secondary language, we will always have a common dialect, the Lord willing."

The Council agreed, though all knew Nimrod had veto power in his kingdom over things like that. However, with Azurad in the mix, they figured her father would relent eventually. After sanctioning Eber's family as the sole guardians of *Adamic*, the Elders sent Peleg – and the Sons of Noah – out to distribute humanity, again.

Eber's family had sorted out their directions long ago. Peleg and his tribe would continue to live in Ur, where he could help Arpa, continue to operate his business, and monitor the Second Sending, which was mostly out of his control by then anyway.

To fill his newly found spare time, Peleg developed an innovative way of rotating crops around the fields on Arpa's farm. It significantly slowed the salinization of the soil, which revitalized crops such as wheat in the south.

Joktan's family returned to Harran. Their fields required tending and the children needed to get back into a routine. Joktan proved his worth by expanding the family's product mix, thanks to a new irrigation system based on his brother's design.

It allowed them to move into crops normally imported from the south, such as melons, cucumbers, and oranges.

Harran had become their home, so the familiarity was comforting after the chaos of Babylon. Azurad spent weeks fussing over their cottage while Eber puttered making minor repairs. Once friends and family learned they had returned, a steady stream of people came by to see them.

Among the visitors were Abram, and Sarah – with Eliezer trailing behind them. After greeting the others, Azurad spent a long time hugging her brother, and later they talked for hours sitting outside under the stars.

Eliezer encouraged Azurad to befriend Sarah. Both were struggling with depression at the time – Sarah over being childless so late in life, and Azurad over what she had seen in Babylon. Faith in the Living God kept both afloat emotionally, and soon they felt comfortable sharing deep feelings that helped both move forward.

The ensuing decades were a time of healing for the entire family, especially with little controversial news coming from the south. Eber's business moving timber to the cities was slow to recover, but eventually rebuilding efforts began to ramp up in Babylon. The volume was not the same as before, but it was enough for them to live comfortably.

Thank you for a time of peace, Eber said to God as he snacked on grapes at his kitchen table one afternoon.

A few minutes later, Azurad burst into their cottage in tears, laid down on their bed, and curled up in fetal position. Eber was not sure what to do next, so he just laid down behind his wife and held her while she sobbed.

After a long 10 minutes, she sat up abruptly and said:

"God wants us to move to Canaan."

***

Eber was beyond confused. Azurad had just named the only disputed territory in the world. They would be leaving their entire support system, including relatives and business networks, for a place where they would be considered foreigners.

Also, God would be taking his wife away from her two most cherished friendships – Eliezer and Sarah. And finally, Eber's body felt way too old for a major move like that.

When Azurad stopped sobbing, she explained the Companion had appeared to her, with an angel on each side. He talked about how God wanted to help the Sons of Shem reclaim land ordained for them. When Azurad asked how that could happen, the Companion said, "The answer to that is in your husband's name."

Eber's name had dual meanings – "to cross over" and "one from beyond." Azurad was unclear how either applied yet, but when staring at 10-foot-tall angels neither logic nor doctrine mattered much.

One thing she did know: God had walked with them through every hard thing so far, so she trusted him. If the Lord wanted her family in Canaan, it was to build a future there.

Still, crossing over into a new place as an outsider would not be easy, so Eber and Azurad agreed to spend a week fasting, praying, and talking candidly.

Why would God send them so late in life? Neither was overly enthused about taking on something like that when much younger family members were available. However, in the end, they agreed it was clear direction from God they needed to follow, no matter how difficult.

Azurad had supported Eber over the Tower prophecy, and now it was his turn to support her.

Making the decision to move was hard enough. Walking it out became a complicated ordeal. Just packing took weeks. Eber and Azurad gathered all their family, servants, possessions, livestock, food, and water. Then they loaded up camels and wagons for the long journey to Canaan.

***

When they left Harran, the farewell was deeply emotional for the entire family. Azurad cried for weeks ahead of time. Joktan and his wife disappeared for a few days to process what was happening. Joktan's sons were especially upset, because they had established a strong bond with Eber over decades.

After they finished loading up wagons and hooking up their beasts of burden, the family hugged and wept openly, again. Azurad desperately clung to her little brother, knowing the chances of seeing him again were slim.

Eber was more frustrated than sad. He had rationalized everything up to that point, but he bitterly complained to God about being sent away from long-time friends he loved – including true believers like Sarah and Abram – on a mission with no clear objective, yet again.

This was just another example of how God's plan seemed so elusive to Eber. For example, Abram had talked about receiving a vision that he would be father to many nations, but that was hard to take seriously when he was old and childless. And it seemed like Eber was always having to deal with loss.

When will the Sending end? Eber asked God. *Why can't you keep us where my wife and I are happy?*

The Second Sending had seemed sensible during the Great Confusion, but at times Eber had second thoughts about dividing and dispersing his core family.

Arpa had told stories about how difficult it was to survive in the First Sending. Nobody had planted fields or vineyards yet, and game was scarce, so they often sought shelter in caves – even while cities were being built. It was a harsh and unforgiving existence at times.

Eber felt like they were in the same place now, and it seemed like a step backward. The saving grace had been the fact the Companion was leading them down the road, with Azurad close behind walking at her normal double-time pace.

"We can always come back if things don't work out there," Eber blurted out as Harran disappeared over a ridgeline.

Azurad turned her head, glared at her husband, turned back, and picked up her pace. Eber realized he had been insensitive, but there was no point trying to apologize at that moment.

The journey was long, strenuous, and at times an endless series of rocky hills. Their welcome in Canaan was warm and gracious, but it quickly became obvious they were among a small minority. The family mostly kept to itself, settling into the routines of farming and animal care. That helped to take their minds off the fact their friends and family were so far away.

Also, Peleg and Joktan connected Eber with the expanding trade network now running from Damascus to the City of Salem. That enabled the family to stay in touch with events in Harran and the southern cities.

About five years after moving to Canaan, Eber was meeting with former colleagues at his home and took a break in the afternoon to get some refreshments. He led the other men outside into their small courtyard, which had a table set up with a variety of bread, cheeses, fruit, and wine under the shade of a grape trellis. Eber heard Azurad burst from the cottage laughing.

He turned to see her leading a happy group of young women, wearing a bright apron and carrying a large bowl. She looked at Eber, then seemed to look beyond him. Azurad dropped the bowl and began to run – directly past the table where Eber was sitting and down the hill toward the road.

Several people were approaching their cottage. They looked familiar, but Eber was having trouble seeing their faces. When it hit him, he jumped to his feet. Abram, Sarah, and Eliezer were walking toward a joyful Azurad.

Eber wondered how they ended up in Canaan, but it was not important. The Companion was leading them, so he followed Azurad down the hill and tried to keep up.

12

The Restoration

When Eber walked out of his farmhouse in the hills near Bethel for the last time, he did not expect anyone to be sending him off – much less about 100 people.

A bustling mix of relatives, friends, dignitaries, and area elders fussed over him. Eber thought it was all unnecessary, since he already had said good-bye to everyone who mattered, if they weren't dead already.

True, he had lived in Canaan for hundreds of years, but who remembered him from the time of the Second Sending? So much had happened since then, but now it was time to move back home to Ur, where he could spend his final years tending the family farm in a much warmer location.

The long trip south just amplified his nostalgia, serving as a memory tablet of Eber's life and triggering a flood of images in his mind – some too painful to dwell on.

It started when they reached the cutoff to Harran. He could see the northeast mountains and thought of Noah. Eber wondered if he would have had the strength to lead his family down from high peaks like those – at *any* age.

From here, Eber's family had taken the road north to Harran decades ago when they moved from Ur to evade participating in Nimrod's Tower project. Abram – later renamed Abraham – and Sarah had come to the same crossroads heading southwest from Harran, toward a land they had never seen based on promise that they would produce a great nation. At the time, he was 75 and she was 65 with no children of their own.

Why does God have a thing about calling people late in life to do the impossible? Eber wondered with a chuckle.

Despite the melancholy of the trip, Eber saw encouraging signs outside the cities – especially in how nature was recovering from the Day of Destruction. After a difficult five-year famine, which Peleg attributed to poison ash from the Tower that had rained over a 200-mile radius, the plants and animals recovered faster than humans expected, yet again.

Date and fig trees had become productive after years of being barren. Oil palm trees began to develop fronds again. But most important, olive trees finally bloomed.

The painful olive oil shortage had taken everyone by surprise, because nearly every household had a grove of short, gnarled olive trees nearby. When all stopped producing drupes at once, there was nothing to harvest, press, or seal. After the trees failed to bud for two years in a row, supplies shrank to black-market levels, causing the price of oil to soar.

Almost overnight, olive oil transformed from being a ubiquitous commodity to its own currency. Worse, the First Babylonian Famine exposed a collective dependency for the oil.

For centuries, olive oil had been important in preparing and cooking foods. However, because it was so abundant, olive oil also had become a key ingredient in making sacred oils for most religious activities. As a result, people began hoarding it early in the famine.

Anyone who had a surplus of olive oil heading into the crisis made a fortune on mark-ups over ensuing years. At the height of the oil shortage, one of the big winners was Nanna International, which sold small jars of "Ancient Remedy" brand oils in their temple lobby stores at exorbitant prices.

Anointing oil that had been blessed by the Lord Priestess could cost a year's wages.

As Eber stood at the intersection of roads leading to either Harran or Ur, two cities that had been so important in his life, the oil crisis seemed long ago.

He leaned against his staff and thought: *Come to think of it, that actually* was *a long time ago.*

The concept got funnier the longer he thought about it, until he was laughing out loud. He had not been that amused when oil prices plummeted, because he guessed wrong on the timing and lost money.

There was no guesswork this day, however. As planned, they went south along the Great River toward the Gulf, following the trade route Eber had helped to develop – especially the familiar commercial cities of Mari, Sippar, Babylon, Erech, and finally his hometown of Ur.

***

The last time Eber had been in the City of Ur was for Arpa's memorial service. That was almost 100 years ago, yet he still missed his grandfather's perspective. It had been especially valuable in their final conversation, during the darkest period in Eber's life – shortly after the death of his beloved Azurad.

As one of the last "Ancient Ones" who lived at least 400 years, Eber had accepted early that nobody would remember him. After all, most of the people he knew were born more than 300 years after his dream about the Tower. And most of what he accomplished in his career was long forgotten, even by himself.

Knowing his life expectancy, Eber had anticipated outliving people he loved. He just did not expect to outlive them *all.*

Of course, the most painful loss had been Azurad. Even thinking about his wife still brought tears.

Eber was coping better than expected, because he was comfortable with being alone. Azurad also had been fine on her own, and that was part of their success in marriage. He had to travel on a regular basis, which meant they would have weeks apart – missing, appreciating, and trusting each other. On the other hand, she often would join him on longer trips.

However, during her final year, Azurad battled a mysterious illness that sapped her strength and required Eber to stay close to home. Azurad gradually lost her appetite and weight, developed severe discomfort in her abdomen, and barely had enough energy to get out of bed.

Azurad's spirits were boosted by the arrival of Sarah, who immediately became a daily presence in their home. After Terah died, God had directed Abraham and Sarah to leave Harran and move to Canaan. They obeyed. After loading up their servants and children, nephew Lot, every possession they owned, herds and flocks, and a small group of followers, they headed west.

Sarah later admitted to Azurad that she had been relieved to leave Harran. She had grown weary of the continual gossiping among the women in her husband's camp, especially over the fact Sarah was childless in her 60s. She also did not miss the constant pressure to attend ostentatious temple events, preferring her garden during the day and reading in the evening.

The friendship between Azurad and Sarah was rich and deep. They shared a love for three things – God, hospitality, and children. In fact, Azurad insisted on hosting friends a week before she died, even though she was in great pain.

Sarah was always there to help. The first day of her return, it felt as if they had never been apart. And on her deathbed, Azurad told Sarah the great joy of her final years had been reuniting. It was understandable, since the two women shared a friendship that spanned a century and three cities thousands of miles apart.

After Azurad died, Sarah came by less, until eventually she became just occasional news from other family members.

Abraham and his family settled in Bethel, but a famine had forced them into Egypt. Later they moved up to the semi-desert Negev area in the south, where Abraham apparently became quite wealthy raising livestock and trading silver.

Eventually they returned to Bethel, but their flocks and herds were so large that he and Lot decided to split their animals and move them into separate grazing lands.

Lot chose the Jordan River plain, and it did not go well.

At one point his family got caught in the middle of a regional war – five city kings against four. The king of Sodom was on the losing end, and the city was plundered. In the process Lot's family and all their possessions were carried off.

It could have been worse for them. Many of the farmer-soldiers from Sodom died gruesome deaths while fleeing into the Valley of Siddim, not realizing it was replete with large pits of flammable liquid bitumen oozing from underground.

When Abraham learned of the battle, he showed his leadership by quickly mustering a militia of 318 trained men. They marched all night, defeated the kings, then returned Lot and everything he owned to his home in Sodom City.

Eber stopped and stared at the ground. He did not want to think about that awful city – especially the day he watched sulfur rain down on it. The scene reminded him too much of what he had seen in Babylon so long ago, and the images from *that* disaster still haunted him. Fortunately, nobody asked him to join the rescue teams heading to Sodom and Gomorrah because he was over 300 years old by then.

***

Eber's world did not intersect with Abraham again until three years after Sarah died. He was sitting on his porch having lunch with a neighbor when a tall, lanky man approached. Eber looked closer, then gasped.

It was Eliezer. A young woman and two men followed him up the path, and the Companion was close behind.

Eber embraced his brother-in-law for a long time. Then Eliezer raised his hands toward heaven and thanked God for blessing him with family. Eber was grateful for the much-needed gift of someone with memories of Azurad.

Over the next few hours, Eliezer told one amazing story after another of what God had done. It had begun with the birth of Isaac, the "Miracle Baby" who was born when Abraham was 100 and Sarah was 90. Isaac had ushered in a series of peaceful years, with the boy being mentored on the ways of the Lord by Noah, Shem, and the rest of the family.

However, when it was time for Isaac to find a wife, his parents were not comfortable with him marrying a local Canaanite woman. Most of them came from polytheistic families that worshiped false gods and practiced rituals such as child sacrifice. In fact, Sarah's final request had been for her son to obtain a wife from their relatives back in Harran.

By then Abraham was too old to travel that far, and Isaac had to manage a family business that had grown too large to leave for months. The solution was to send Eliezer to Harran.

Abraham trusted his chief servant so much he gave him the task of finding a wife for his son.

"I'd like you to meet Rebekah, daughter of your relative Bethuel," Eliezer said. "I brought her from Harran to Canaan to marry Abraham's son."

***

A beautiful young woman stepped forward, bowed respectfully, greeted Eber in the name of the Living God, and said how much she had been looking forward to meeting him.

"I would love to learn for myself why our family has started calling itself the Sons of Eber, great father," she said.

Her kind greeting and the strong presence of the Companion by her side caused Eber's face to transform from a pale sadness to bright smile. However, her formal salutation simply would not do, so he stepped forward, gave Rebekah an affectionate hug, and warmly welcomed her to the family.

Over the next few hours, they sat at a table having lunch while Eliezer recounted the incredible way in which he met Rebekah. Eber listened carefully, enjoying every detail.

When Eliezer left Canaan, he had loaded 10 camels with gifts and goods, then set out for an area outside Harran where their relatives lived. It was a long journey, but he wasted no time once there. In fact, he did not even go all the way into the city. Eliezer stopped at a well just outside the town wall and prayed for help.

The result was a divine encounter with Rebekah and her family. By the next morning, they were heading to Canaan.

"The *next* morning?" Eber asked with a laugh. "How did her mother take that?"

"She tried to stall us," Eliezer said, "but I was pretty focused and insisted on leaving immediately."

The family eventually capitulated after they brought out Rebekah and asked her opinion. She looked at Eliezer and said simply, "I will go."

Azurad would have loved this woman, Eber thought.

Eliezer told how the entire family had gathered to say goodbye, on a gloomy day in Harran with overcast skies and a steady rain. As their caravan slowly wound around a bend in the path heading toward the Great River, Rebekah looked back and saw most of her family still standing in the rain weeping. She turned to look forward and began softly singing "The Rainbow Promise."

As Eliezer finished his story, Eber realized God was doing something extraordinary, yet again. But he also knew from experience it would exact a great cost.

Every generation has its Day of Reckoning. For Eber, it was never about historic events. His greatest struggle had been over Azurad's disease and death. He spent many hours begging God for his wife's life. Instead, she kept getting sicker, and he kept getting more bitter.

His attitude changed one day near the end when Azurad unexpectedly sat up and thanked him for being her husband.

"You have been the heart of my heart since I was a child, Eber," she said. "But you need to let me return to the Creator. I am ready to cross over, my love. You have helped many in our family move beyond pain to restoration.

"Now it is my turn."

Eber began to protest, but Azurad gently put her fingers on his lips, and soon both were soaked in tears. He crawled onto the bed, laid down behind her, pulled up a blanket, and held her.

Eber and Azurad lay quietly basking in the comfort of their love for a final hour. Eventually, Azurad breathed her last, as the Companion wept in the corner.

No one tried to console Eber. His loss was beyond comprehension. More than two centuries of shared experiences, beginning in childhood, could never be replaced. Unfortunately, Azurad's death was just the beginning of an extended period of loss that almost became too much for Eber to bear.

Next came the unexpected death of Peleg. Though he was 239 years old, Eber's oldest son had been a rock in the family for so long he would be impossible to replace.

That was followed too quickly by Joktan. Over ensuing decades, Eber even had to attend multiple funerals for beloved great-grandchildren, which felt surreal and unnatural.

Despite that, Eber was at peace with the fact he might be the last one standing in his generation. After all, Noah died at age 600, Arpa at 438, and Shelah at 433. However, reality hit Eber hard at the memorial service for Shem.

The son of Noah lived 600 years, mostly in obscurity, so few people even remembered his great-grandchildren, much less Shem himself. As a result, only 12 people attended his low-key memorial service.

***

The final blow was the death of Abraham at age 175, when Eber was 460. As he sat at the memorial service held by Abraham's sons Isaac and Ishmael at the cave of Machpelah, Eber found himself looking around at a sea of faces he did not recognize. At that moment, he knew it was time to go home.

His family had lived in Harran and Canaan for centuries, but his roots were in the south, so returning to Ur and its more favorable weather was a sensible decision – emotionally as well as physically.

Ur had become Eber's sanctuary over the years, mostly because Arpa had lived there for so long. His cottage was the site of many life-shaping conversations. Their final talk there, the day after Shelah's funeral, had been especially poignant.

Eber was at a low point and bitter at the time. He had lost most of the people he loved, including Azurad. He had battled false religions his entire life, watched thousands of people die, had to start over from scratch in a foreign land late in life, and could see little evidence that God cared about him anymore.

Arpa took Eber outside and raised his hands toward a sky full of stars over the Gulf.

"*There* is the evidence he cares," Arpa said. "He is much bigger than our problems, my grandson. I have seen him in a sunrise atop the Cliffs of Najaf and in a sunset over the Great Sea. The Living God does not dwell in buildings made by people.

"Heaven is all around, Eber. But to see it, you must view the world from God's perspective. He showed you that in your Tower dream as a boy."

***

Eber was startled at the mention of his dream. At that point, Arpa was the only other banquet attendee still alive to remember it. Eber always had sensed the dream was more than just about Nimrod, but he had given up hope of ever understanding it fully.

Nimrod had seen the Tower as proof he was a god. The destruction of the Tower was ample evidence the king was, in fact, mortal. As a result, most interpretations of the dream now seemed convoluted at best. Arpa understood it clearly.

"The dream was for you personally, but also for the family of God," Arpa said during their last conversation. "Over time, you shed things that were unnecessary distractions to your walk with God. Each time it happened, your life gained fresh focus and simplicity. You finally rose above things of this world by looking at life through his eyes instead of your own.

"You learned it was never necessary to *earn* access to the Creator. He was with you all along. And that was his original design, Eber. Your descendants will cross over into a new covenant with the Lord – and that one will restore *all* things."

Arpa turned with a determined look and nodded his head. The Companion stood next to him, nodding in agreement.

***

The hill leading to the ridge overlooking the City of Ur seemed longer and steeper than Eber remembered, but he expected it at his age, *400-something*.

Two young men walked on either side, helping to steady him on the rocky sections. Eber had made sure to remember their names, but their family connection through 10 generations was fuzzy at best.

Everybody else is a great-great something when you live this long, he thought.

Eber paused to look at the Gulf now a skim on the southern horizon. The landscape looked so familiar, yet so foreign.

Arpa had often talked about the amount of change that occurred in in a compressed period after The Deluge. It created opportunities but also caused severe problems. Cities and towers had come and gone. Humans had invented writing, mathematics, music, new types of metal alloys, canals that made deserts flourish, and much more.

However, in the race for new technologies they destroyed the environment with no regard for future generations. People also created new gods to meet selfish needs, and with enthusiasm. Eber's own family had been among them.

Laughter drew him from his reverie. His two young companions were on the ground wrestling over an apple. How long ago had it been since he had roamed the land playing with his band of brothers?

Eber stopped to rest at the familiar crest overlooking the Gulf. He leaned on his staff, closed his eyes, and soaked in the comforting breeze of the Companion's presence. By now, Eber did not have to look to know he was there. It was an odd sensation of being alone, but not lonely. Since the Azurad's death, the Companion had been with him every day.

"Do you remember what I asked the last time we talked?" the Companion asked.

Eber thought for a moment. "You asked what had changed most since meeting you," he said. "Certainly, the world is much different. But I think my heart has changed most."

Years ago, that would have sounded trite and self-serving, even to Eber. Today, it was simply true.

Many in Eber's family worshiped multiple gods, so he had been proselytized from an early age and from multiple directions. Most of the temples were sincere, with law-abiding adherents who had high moral standards, were involved in their communities, and helped others with compassion.

They just lacked one thing: In all the religions Eber had encountered, he had found only one *real* God.

For some reason, the Creator of all things had pursued Eber since childhood. Often it had felt intensely personal, so from a young age he felt a need to earn his way into heaven.

However, paradise always felt like a shifting target. When Eber realized he could *never* be good enough, he fell into years of despair and self-condemnation. All that changed when Azurad comforted Eber just before her death – at a time when he should have been supporting *her*.

"You have always been too hard on yourself, my dear," Azurad said. "Heaven is not about how good *we* are, but rather how good *he* is."

The truth that God's love could restore him was liberating, and it lifted a long-standing load of guilt off Eber's heart. At that moment he realized the goal had never been heaven. The goal was God himself. And he had never been far away. In fact, he was standing next to him *wanting* to be a daily companion.

Heaven was a final resting place, but not the desire of Eber's heart after that. The only thing he wanted now was to be with God. If that was in heaven, great. If that was out feeding the poor, comforting widows, or visiting prisoners, even better.

If God was there, nothing else mattered.

***

Eber gazed at the landscape he first saw as a young man. It had gone from lush marshland to a wasteland, then nature had reversed the process and reclaimed it as a habitat teaming with wildlife again. That was always God's way – restoration.

Eber looked over at the Companion, who was peacefully leaning against a staff, and deeply appreciated his consistent presence over more than 400 years of wandering.

"Will I ever see heaven?" Eber asked.

The Companion sighed, turned, and said, "Eber, you will enter its gates to great celebration. And God himself will be there to greet you with open arms."

"If I can be bold, what will that be like?" Eber asked.

"It will be your Day of Days," the Companion said. "And that is a promise."

Eber looked toward the sky to thank God, and out of a cloud he saw a rainbow begin to form. It grew wider as it descended until it dropped over the mountains to the east, their destination.

The Companion smiled, eased close to Eber, took his hand, and helped him to his feet. Then they walked arm-in-arm down the hill toward home.

***

ABOUT THE AUTHOR

Stan Johnston loves to sing, write, and dream about the future. Friends and family fed his passion for performing arts early in life, but he decided that music would not be his vocation. After attending the University of Missouri's School of Journalism, he became a sportswriter – covering major events such as the Super Bowl, World Series, and World Cup qualifying. That led to stints as sports editor of *The Sacramento Bee* and *St. Louis Sun,* among others.

However, still a boy at heart, he envisioned a world with flying cars, so he left the newspaper industry for Information Technology. To get there, he became an expert in grown-up topics such as digital content, platforms, and processes. Along the way he also gained a deep understanding of what organizations face in digital transformation. He used those skills to help HP Enterprise, NetApp, McClatchy and other companies grow business in substantive ways.

This dreamer will never outgrow his love for competitive business challenges, robust discussions, and tight harmonies. However, these days he also writes books like this in Pollock Pines, California. Let me know if you would like to meet him: bystanjohnston@gmail.com

CPSIA information can be obtained
at www.ICGtesting.com
Printed in the USA
BVHW040106070421
604344BV00014B/1815